MW01028669

FIRE BEACH

PARADISE CRIME MYSTERIES BOOK 8

TOBY NEAL

Proverbs 14:11
A wise woman builds her house; a foolish woman tears hers down with her own hands.

CHAPTER ONE

"FIRE IS POETRY. FLAME IS DESTINY." The Fireman smiled to himself as he said the words out loud, tasting the way they sounded.

Heading for an ignition site brought that poetic side out in him. Next to him, on the floor of the battered old truck, a rusty gas can rattled as he drove down the deserted sugarcane-hauling road. Harsh red dust rose from the potholed dirt as Maui's strong trade winds kicked up.

He'd chosen a cane field they'd be burning in a week or two, yellowing since the company'd stopped watering it, fifteen-foot flowering tassels of mature sugarcane waving like mares' tails. But if he burned it first, the cane company would lose their harvest, two years of work, and thousands of dollars.

The Fireman pulled the dust-covered truck over at one of the points of origin he'd chosen. He splashed the area with a mix of diesel to cling to the sugarcane, plus gas for ignitability, and tossed a match. He jumped back into the truck, feeling that kick of adrenaline, and floored it to the next ignition site, where he repeated the process. And a third time.

The Fireman looked back down the road into the wall of rising flames. It was catching faster than he'd planned. Maybe this one would jump the highway, really put a thrill into the Road to Hana for the tourists.

He stood there and savored a feeling of power as crackling energy released all around him. The sweet-smelling, burnt-sugar smoke soared into the higher elevations and hit colder air, coalescing into mushroom-cloud shapes. White cattle egrets flew in, landing in the road to feast on fleeing insects. A familiar roaring filled his ears as the heat fanned his cheeks.

The fire was a creature of beauty. He extended a hand to the fire, enjoying the multisensory experience he'd unleashed—and a back swirl of wind blew a tongue of flame to sear that hand like the lash of a whip. He howled in pain and hurled the gas can he was still holding into the oncoming inferno before it could blow up in his hand.

He leaped into the truck, threw it into gear, and peeled away. He couldn't help ducking as the gas can exploded behind him with a *boom!* He floored it and pulled away, bouncing crazily down the potholed dirt road toward the highway. He lifted his hand, seared across the back in a stripe that looked like raw steak.

He licked the burn, tasting ash and blood. "Bitch. How I love you."

Behind his racing truck, the wall of flame swept forward into the field with a crackling scream like a thousand demons in chorus. Insects, birds, mongooses, and more fled in futile terror before it.

Lieutenant Michael Stevens picked up a call at his office in Haiku. "Bro, it's Jared." His little brother's voice sounded amped up and hoarse. "I thought I'd better call you. You know that cane fire this morning?"

Jared was a firefighter at Kahului Station, recently transferred to Maui to get away from the holocaust of summer fires in LA—but from what Stevens could tell, Maui hadn't been the mellow posting Jared was hoping for.

"Yeah, I saw the smoke. Smelled it, too. Thought they were just doing a scheduled burn." Maui was one of the last places in the United States still growing and harvesting sugar. The plantation operated at an annual loss, in part because of the vast amount of water and resources it took to produce even a single pound of "white gold." The harvesting process was also pollution-heavy. It began with burning fields to get rid of excess leaves, leaving the stalks behind, heavy with syrup, to be processed.

"No. We think it's another arson case." Jared coughed. "We've almost got it contained. Remember, I told you there have been at least three of these arson cane fires in the last month. Anyway, there's a fatality. Tourists found a guy on the side of the road, crispy as a chicken wing."

Stevens winced inwardly, trying not to imagine what "crispy as a chicken wing" looked like in human form. Likely he'd get to see firsthand. He stood, reaching for the shoulder holster hung on the wall to strap into. "So if it was arson, it's a homicide."

"Right. I thought I'd give you a heads-up since it's in your district."

As if on cue, his radio crackled with the call to respond. "Thanks, Jared. If I don't see you at the scene, I'll see you at dinner tonight. Still coming, right?"

"Right. I'll bring dessert." Jared had begun making weekly visits to have dinner with Stevens, his pregnant wife, Lei Texeira, their son, Kiet, and Lei's dad, Wayne, who lived with them and provided child care.

Stevens hung up and stuck his head outside his office to holler to his veteran detective. "Ferreira! Ten-fifty on Hana Highway!"

They got on the road in Stevens's brown Bronco, cop light strobing on the dash. Ferreira, a middle-aged man of portly build and grizzled visage, worked the radio, getting as much information as he could. "Ambulance is there. Too late, but at least they can keep the lookie-loos away."

"How far is the vic from the fire?"

"On the edge of the highway. Fire burned up to the road, like they usually do. Fire department is working on keeping it from spreading."

"This will add more tension to the whole no-burn movement," Stevens said thoughtfully, rubbing the tiny purple heart tattoo in the crook of his elbow with a thumb as he drove. A vocal faction on the island had begun protesting the traditional method of harvest, citing asthma and a host of environmental concerns.

"I don't see how this has anything to do with that," Ferreira said, frowning. "These burns are just some misguided kids making trouble. Don't see how arson that's just killed a man has anything to do with the burns the cane company does for harvest—something they've been doing for a hundred years."

"Okay. I hope you're right." Stevens knew Ferreira was from a big family that had come over to Hawaii in one of the original immigration waves, working their way up from the "cane camp" shantytowns to powerful positions in local government and solid occupation of the middle class. He'd heard Ferreira lament the demise of sugarcane agriculture in Maui often enough not to argue with the man. He also knew proponents of the change to machine harvesters would make the argument that drying the fields in preparation for controlled burning provided tempting targets for arson.

They sped down the winding two-lane highway that followed the windswept coastline. Even responding to a call and driving at top speed, Stevens sneaked a few looks out his window at the ocean, a tapestry of blues from cobalt to the palest turquoise at the foam-flecked shore. Surfers, windsurfers, and kiteboarders all played along this coastline, and the colorful sails leaping over the waves reminded him of darting butterflies.

The fire was still smoldering in the charred field as they came around a corner to where barricades had been set up, diverting traffic along an old road that connected above the beach town of Paia. Stevens pulled up and parked the Bronco, snapping on gloves and picking up his crime kit. Ferreira did the same.

"Booties would be good," Ferreira said, slipping on a pair of blue elastic-edged, fabric shoe covers.

"Good idea. Though I'm not sure how well these are going to

hold up on this ground," Stevens said, looking at the still-smoking rubble that lined the road.

Just as Jared had told him, the fire had burned up to the highway, eating everything in its path down to the black ribbon of road. The fire zone was very close to the oceanfront community of Kuau, a cluster of residences along the coast. Stevens had spent the last year before his marriage to Lei at a little apartment in Kuau and had an affection for the ragtag collection of older plantation-style homes interspersed with oceanfront mansions.

They walked down the road and approached the body, draped in a white cloth that was staining in patches from body fluids.

The medical examiner, Dr. Gregory, had beaten them to the scene. Squatted beside the body, he was wearing an aloha shirt decorated with cartoon menehunes, attention fixed on the grisly sight before him.

There was an unpleasant, oily quality to the smoked-barbecue odor of the body as Stevens inadvertently sniffed the air. He was glad Lei hadn't had to go out on this call. At four months pregnant, his wife's worst symptom seemed to be an oversensitivity to smells. This stench would definitely have had her running for the nearest toilet.

"Ah, Lieutenant," Dr. Gregory said, looking up. Magnifying glasses made him look like a bug until he pushed the optics up onto his reddened forehead. "Got a few interesting things about this body."

Stevens gave a nod to Ferreira to go find the fire investigator. They'd be relying heavily on the fire department's assessment of the evidence found at the burn site. He squatted beside Dr. Gregory as the man uncovered the body further. Bits of clothing and skin clung to the sheet. "I wish they wouldn't have covered the body with this," the ME fussed. "Contaminating the trace here."

"So this is what human barbecue looks like," Stevens said. "Not pretty." He'd seen burn victims before, but not since he'd moved to Hawaii five years ago.

"Not pretty at all. Check out the feet."

Stevens looked. The toes were burned, the feet curled as tendons retracted. "No shoes?"

"Exactly. I wonder if that's significant."

Stevens looked around the corpse. He didn't see anything beside the body, nor marks on the ground. "Guess he collapsed here from the smoke and then the fire got him."

"I think he was running and was on fire," Gregory said. "His feet are more burned than his hands, and the back of his clothing is completely gone."

Stevens tried not to imagine the man's terrible death, instead focusing on his next steps. "Did you check for ID in his pockets?"

"I need to go over the whole body at the lab," Gregory said. "The cloth that's left is burned right onto his skin. Anything still on him will be degrees of melted. I need to keep it all clean and preserved. Anything else you need here? Because I'd like to bag him."

"Are the fire investigators done?"

"We should check." Gregory radioed, and a young man moving with athletic grace in spite of heavy fire-retardant gear broke away from a knot of firefighters and came their way.

"Tim Owen. Fire investigator for the County of Maui." He introduced himself, and Stevens shook his gauntleted hand.

"Lieutenant Stevens. You already know Dr. Gregory."

"Yes."

"I want to bag the body, Tim," Gregory said. "Need anything more?"

"No. I'm still determining the point of origin, though directionality of the char pattern makes me think it started somewhere on the cane-haul road. This guy was somewhere in this field when it went up. Maybe a homeless guy, sleeping in the cane. No shoes makes me think so."

"So what did the body tell you?" Dr. Gregory asked. Stevens thought he might be testing the fire investigator's assessment.

"Wasn't trapped in the flames for an extended period—see, the arms are in fairly good shape." Owen pointed out the folded, crabbed arms. "His face is even recognizable. The feet are worked over, but they were exposed. Maybe he ran across some burning area with bare feet. Beneath the body, he's got fabric intact. So my take is the fire woke him up, but he was probably dazed from smoke. These cane fires burn fast, and he wasn't moving quickly enough. He collapsed here, and the fire flashed over him. Burned a while in this spot, enough to cook his feet pretty good."

Gregory nodded. "That was my initial take, too."

"We don't get many vagrants or homeless sleeping in the cane," Stevens said. "Lots of spiders in there." The cane spiders were famous in Hawaii. Hairy and brown, with long, slender legs, they grew to be six to eight inches in diameter and dominated their home in the sugarcane. "The cane is sharp and dense. Not much squatting happens in there between the spiders and the leaves being sharp enough to cut you."

"Seems like that's a good thing. I'm new here. I'm just getting the 'lay of the land,' so to speak, but I'm already concerned about all these arson fires. Makes me think someone's targeting the sugarcane company."

"Could be," Stevens said. "Do you have any interviews set up with them?"

"Matter of fact, I do. Tomorrow morning, talking with upper management at the Puunene Mill, to see if they have any idea about who might have it in for them." Owen wiped his sweaty face with a bandanna, and Stevens could see how young he was. New to the island, he might not get that far talking to the locals without support.

"Well, now that this is a homicide case, how about Ferreira and I tag along?"

"That would be great." Stevens didn't think he was imagining the note of relief in the young man's voice. "Can't understand the pidgin when people get going."

Ferreira stepped up and stuck out his hand. "Know a lot of people at the company. I can help."

"Excellent."

They exchanged details for the next morning's meeting while Dr. Gregory and Tanaka, his assistant, got the body bagged with the help of the EMTs who had come out on the call. Stevens was relieved when the body, still reeking even in the bag, was on the way to the morgue.

Human barbecue wasn't something he ever wanted to see again. A bad feeling clung to him, along with the smell.

CHAPTER TWO

Lᴇɪ Tᴇxᴇɪʀᴀ ᴅʀᴏᴠᴇ up the winding two-lane road through rural Haiku on Maui's north shore. Tall eucalyptus trees, giant tree ferns, wandering vines, and bright sprays of ginger and heliconia bordered the road. It was a mellow thirty-minute drive from her workplace, Maui Police Station in downtown Kahului, to the home she and Stevens had bought in the countryside. Her flagging afternoon energy, another pregnancy symptom, lifted as she turned up the gravel driveway. Coming home always did that for her, especially now that her father, Wayne, had moved to Maui and was taking care of baby Kiet during the day.

Their new house was set back from the road behind an automatic gate. She hit the buttons and retracted it. The fence around the property was ten feet high, made of cedar, and it provided both protection and privacy. Keiki, her battle-scarred Rottweiler, greeted the truck with happy barks and ran alongside as she drew up to the house.

"New" wasn't actually the right word for the house. It was fifty years old, surrounded by fruit-bearing trees and built in the sprawling plantation-style she and Stevens loved. It had been added on to so that the original footage had multiplied. Still, the size and acreage would have made it an impossible investment for a young couple just starting out if Lei's Aunty Rosario hadn't left them her bungalow in California as an inheritance. Wayne had helped them sell it after Aunty's recent death in order to buy the house, and now they carried a small, manageable mortgage. The property even had a small *ohana* cottage, where Wayne lived.

Lei pulled into the open garage, beeped the truck locked, and went up the steps to the security door. "Hey, Dad," she called, unlocking the steel-grilled door. Even out here in the country, they weren't safe. An unknown enemy they'd taken to calling the 'shroud killer' was still at large, continuing to threaten them through the mail after leaving lengths of linen at the deaths of Lei's aunt and Stevens's ex-wife, Anchara. Until he was found, they needed to take every precaution.

"Hey, Sweets," her dad called from the kitchen. "He's excited to see you." Lei heard baby Kiet yell, "Ba-ba-ba!"

"I'm coming!" Lei exclaimed, slipping her shoes off onto the rack beside the front door. "Let me just drop off my weapon." She padded quickly to the bedroom, draped the shoulder holster over the headboard of the king-sized bed, emptying her badge and accoutrements into a basket on the side table. She and Stevens were going to have to start locking up their weapons soon, but they had a few months more until Kiet began crawling around and getting into everything—and soon they'd have a second baby to manage as well.

Lei was eager to take a shower, but Kiet was waiting. She hurried across the polished wood floor of the living room to the kitchen and broke into a smile at the sight of her stepson in his baby carrier on the table, waving his hands, one tooth shining like a pearl in the big grin he gave her.

"Who's my handsome boy?" She smiled into Kiet's jade-dark, smoky green eyes. His shock of black hair always stood on end, and it quivered like a rooster's tail as she unstrapped him. The baby immediately grabbed her curls with both hands, giggling as she lifted him and blew on his tummy. He kicked his legs and giggled some more, and she hugged him close, turning to her father. "He's in a good mood, Dad."

Wayne was checking something on the stove. By the smell, she guessed it was teriyaki chicken. "He's had a great day. Now that the tooth is out, he's back to being our happy boy."

Lei put the baby on her hip and took one of his chubby hands in hers, then pretended to waltz around the kitchen. Kiet squawked with excitement.

"Don't get him too riled up before dinner, or he'll spit up. Remember what happened last time," Wayne said.

"Oh yeah." Lei snuggled her face into Kiet's delicious neck and blew, and he giggled again. "I'll calm down. I have to go shower anyway, in a minute."

"He's not going to want to let you out of his sight."

"Is that so?" Lei swung Kiet around in front of her, and he laughed again.

"I'll give him his bath in the sink. That'll distract him." Wayne turned on the water.

"Until Daddy gets home," Lei said. Stevens had a different way with Kiet than she did, but the baby seemed to enjoy being with his dad just as much.

Wayne ran the sink full of warm water, and Lei undressed the baby, stripping off his onesie and diaper. Wayne, his smile indulgent, checked the water temperature with his wrist and gestured for Lei to bring him over.

"Come on in. The water's fine, little man," he said, taking his grandchild, but the minute Kiet's feet touched the water, the baby drew them up against his body, squinching his face. "Oh, not warm enough?" Wayne added more hot water, holding the baby close.

Lei left them sorting that out and went back to the bathroom off the master bedroom. She showered, and as she did these days, checked in with the changes in her body. Her breasts were a size larger and tender, and her belly had a fullness to it that had tightened the waistband of her jeans. Another thing no one had told her about pregnancy—how taut her uterus would be, like she was growing a coconut in there. Other than occasional nausea and an acute reaction to smells, Lei felt great.

It was a strange feeling that her body knew what to do all on its own. She still felt surprised that this was the direction her life had gone—marriage, motherhood, living in a house with her dad as the "manny"—but she couldn't imagine another life now. The grief that she wasn't sharing this with her beloved aunt still came over her in waves, and this time she shut her eyes and turned her face into the flow of water from the shower, letting the sorrow move through her.

She was out of the shower and playing with Kiet out on the porch when Stevens drove up in his brown Bronco. Sitting in the old porch rocking chair, she turned Kiet outward as Stevens got out of the truck. The baby flexed his legs, hopping and leaning toward his father.

"Hey, little man." Stevens came up on the porch, leaning down to kiss the baby. Lei drew back, sniffing, before he could kiss her.

"Yuck. Shower first. Been near a fire?"

"Yeah. You saw the smoke earlier?"

"Sure did. Another cane fire. It was out by the time I passed it."

"Fire caught a body this time. I'll tell you when I'm out of the shower and you'll let me kiss you." He winked as he went inside. Kiet bounced and strained after his father as Stevens disappeared into the house.

Lei spun the baby around. "He'll be back. In the meantime, you'll have to make do with me."

Kiet grinned, grabbing a handful of her hair and putting it in his mouth. She was still detaching it as she made her way back to the kitchen. "Can I help you with anything, Dad?"

"Nope. Tell that husband of yours dinner's ready in fifteen minutes." Wayne was tossing a salad. He'd learned kitchen skills in prison, where he'd been on kitchen duty for years. He prepared healthy meals for the family five nights a week, kept the house picked up, and took care of the baby during the day. Lei insisted on paying him a small salary, and he had his own cottage. So far the arrangement seemed to be working out. As far as Lei was concerned, it was close to perfect, and keeping busy with the baby seemed to be helping Wayne stay distracted from the loss of his sister.

"I'll go tell Stevens," Lei said. She tried to put the baby in his bouncy seat, but he grunted and writhed and arched his back, so she toted him back into the bathroom, opening the shower to say to Stevens, "Dinner in fifteen. Is your brother still coming?"

"Said he was," Stevens said, not turning around. She took a minute to enjoy the view of his long, muscular back as he rinsed his hair under the flow of water. Then Kiet pulled her hair again, and Lei sighed as she turned away. Chances to join Stevens in their oversized shower were few and far between nowadays, with the baby to keep entertained and her father always around.

She heard the *beep-beep-beep* on the control panel by the front door that told her someone had punched in the code and activated the gate—probably Jared. Only a handful of friends had the code. Lei felt her spirits lift—she enjoyed Jared's company, and his presence at their family dinners livened things up.

She walked out onto the porch as Jared drove up in the lifted tan Tacoma he drove, the pipe racks on the truck stacked with his "toys"—a couple of surfboards, a stand-up paddleboard, and a single-man canoe.

"Hey, bro," Lei called as he got out of the vehicle. She held up Kiet's hand and waved it at Jared. Her brother-in-law grinned, walking toward her with the swift grace he shared with Stevens. He had the same height and the same blue eyes, but his features were more regular and chiseled, and he had a leanness that looked whipcord strong. As a firefighter, he spent time working out that Stevens didn't put in. When he wasn't at the station, he was out enjoying the ocean sports of Maui. All that added up to spectacular.

"Hey, sis. Hope you weren't the one cooking," Jared said with that wicked grin that Lei knew had kicked a lot of hearts into overdrive. She pretended to punch him in the rock-hard midsection, and he folded comically, making Kiet laugh, a burbling sound Lei loved.

"You know better than that," Lei said. "Take your nephew, please. He's eating my hair again."

"He has good taste," Jared said. "Hey, buddy." He pried Kiet's hands out of Lei's hair and lifted him up. "How's my favorite future firefighter?"

"He's going into something safe. Like accounting," Stevens called from inside the house. "Stop that evil talk."

Jared grinned again, heading into the house with the baby, and Lei racked her brain for who she could set him up with. Sophie Ang? Her friend was still single, though it had seemed like Sophie had a crush on Alika Wolcott, her MMA fighting coach...Lei tried to imagine her serious FBI tech agent friend with daredevil, fun-loving Jared. They were so different, it just might work.

She followed Jared into the house and helped set the table while Jared and Stevens discussed the fire and the "human chicken wing" found on the side of the road. "What do you think of the new fire investigator? Tim Owen?" Stevens asked.

"Seems to know his fire science. I've taken him out stand-up paddling. Since we're both new to the island, we've been getting out on the ocean together."

"I envy your schedule," Stevens said. It wasn't the first time he'd said that, Lei thought. Maybe the time had come for them to just work the hours they were supposed to—but she doubted either of them would be able to stick with those kinds of resolutions the next time a big case came along.

"Thanks, Dad," Lei said, kissing her father's leathery cheek quickly as she took a large casserole dish from him. "This looks so good. So what about that fire victim? Any ID?"

"No. A John Doe at this point," Stevens said.

"Hey, Mr. Texeira, this looks great!" Jared said, eyeing the food. He'd handed Kiet off to Stevens and now he took the pot of rice from Wayne. "Thanks so much for having me."

"Always room and food for family," Wayne said. "Hope you brought that dessert you promised me last week."

"Oh, yeah, thanks for reminding me. I left it in the truck."

Jared set the pot of rice on the table and took off. Lei quirked a brow at her father. "What's he bringing?"

"Surprise. Let's sit down while the food's hot."

They gathered around the picnic table on the covered back deck, mercifully screened from mosquitoes, and Stevens was able to get Kiet into his seat.

"My turn to feed him tonight," Stevens said.

"His rice cereal's in the microwave," Wayne said, carrying a big wooden bowl of salad past Lei to set on the table as she fetched the baby's bowl of cereal. Jared returned, with something in a brown paper bag that he stowed in the freezer.

They ate, sharing snippets about the day. Jared told them about the rash of arson cane fires. "There've been four of these, as you guys must have seen in the news. But now that there's been a homicide, it takes things up a notch. With you guys working with Tim, I hope we'll get the arsonist sooner rather than later."

Wayne shook his silver-shot, curly head. "Homeless guy had to be pretty desperate, sleeping in a cane field."

"Yeah, I hate even going in them. Kind of claustrophobic, the way the cane grows so high," Lei said. "He was out of luck once the fire started."

"Just what I thought," Stevens replied. "It'll be interesting to see if there's more to it than just in the wrong place at the wrong time." Lei watched him feed Kiet a mouthful of rice cereal with the soft plastic baby spoon. Kiet smacked his thighs in excitement, then flailed his hand in an attempt to catch the spoon. "Catch it with your mouth, little man," Stevens said, smiling as he got another bite into the baby.

Lei put her hand on Stevens's thigh, kneading the muscles there. His patience and tenderness with Kiet made her love him in new ways. But happy scenes like this always reminded her of Anchara,

Kiet's mother and Stevens's ex-wife, who'd been murdered a few months ago. The baby's presence with them was wholly due to tragedy. Her killer had been caught, but Lei still thought there was more to the picture than the man had ever confessed.

But maybe Anchara's killer *had* been the shroud killer. After he was taken into custody, things had gone quiet. For more than four months there had been an escalating series of events, but since the arrest, there had been nothing further. Lei took a bite of salad, wondering if she could get away to her computer after dinner. She had a secret she was working on—and there would be hell to pay if Stevens found out about it.

CHAPTER THREE

"I NEED to do some office work after dinner," Lei said to Stevens. "Can you keep him busy until bedtime?"

"No problem—right, buddy?" Stevens said, getting another spoonful into the baby, who smacked his gums happily.

"I'll see you tomorrow, bright and early," Wayne said, getting up and clearing his plate. "Good night."

"Not staying for dessert?" Jared said. "Let me clear the table and I'll get it."

"Oh yeah." Wayne sat back down. "Wouldn't miss that."

"Give me a few minutes. Let me earn my meal." Jared cleared the table efficiently, and Lei, sipping her glass of water, thought how nice it was that not one of the men in her life had a problem with just doing what needed to be done around the house. She'd heard enough grumbles from Tiare Kaihale, her former partner Pono's wife, not to take it for granted.

Ten minutes later Jared reappeared with a bowl piled with translucent white orbs. Lei bugged her eyes at him. "Are those lychee?"

"Got a tree in the stationhouse yard," Jared said. "Your dad told me to chill them and that they make a great dessert."

"Oh my God, yes!" Lei exclaimed, grabbing one of the delicious bite-sized fruits and popping it into her mouth. Sweet-tart flavor with an exotic fragrance burst across her tongue. She shut her eyes to savor as she chewed, then spit the small brown seed into her palm. "Chilling them really does make them even better."

They dug into the bowl until the lychees were gone. "Aren't you glad I told you those funny-looking fruits were good to eat?" Wayne said. "Soon as I knew what firehouse you were at, I had my eye on getting some off that tree."

"You and everybody else," Jared said. "I had to fight the guys off to get even this many once they were ripe."

Lei had discovered the knobbly red fruit, with its tender white flesh, was a prized delicacy seldom found in stores when she'd tried to buy some.

"Well, I better get to bed. Gotta be back here early in the morning," Wayne said, rising.

She got up and gave him a hug. "Thanks, Dad, for another great dinner."

"Thanks, Wayne," Stevens and Jared echoed. Wayne waved casually as he took his leave, shutting the front door behind him.

"So I better get to my office work. You boys have fun with Kiet," Lei said, feeling a prickle of guilt and suppressing it. "Jared, see you next week—if not sooner."

"Wouldn't miss it," Jared said. "Mike, let's put on the game. Never too early to get Kiet following football."

She left them arguing over which team jersey they should order in Kiet's size.

Kiet's room was right next to theirs, and their home office was on the other side of it. She went inside and closed the door. After a moment of hesitation, she locked it. Stevens would be suspicious if he discovered she'd locked him out, but she'd plead confidentiality on a sensitive case. That was at least partially true.

Lei sat down at her computer, booted it up, and put on earbuds. She worked the knob of the safe under her desk and took out a file, then Skyped one of her friends at the FBI, tech agent Sophie Ang.

"Lei." Sophie's close-cropped, elegant head appeared as she answered the call. She was just as riveting on-screen as in person, her tawny-brown skin glowing on the monitor. "What's new?"

"Nothing much, but I'm getting ready to go to the Big Island on a case. I thought I'd take care of some Chang business when I'm over there," Lei said.

"I'm not sure about this whole thing. Marcella and I were talking about it today, and we're both worried."

"I know." Lei blew out a breath. "But I just don't believe Anchara's killer was the guy behind the shrouds. I don't think we're going to be safe until we have the real shroud killer locked down. With a baby or two to protect, I'm just not willing to sit on my ass until he attacks us again. You don't have to help me. I won't talk to you any more if you want out." She pinched the web of flesh between her thumb and forefinger, an old stress-management technique. It was scary to think of investigating Chang completely solo. Just knowing her friends were there, monitoring from the technology end, had helped.

"No. We just don't want you moving on it until you're sure it's Chang, and so far, I don't have anything on him showing a connection to the shrouds."

Months ago, Anchara's killer had bought three shrouds—and only two of them had been accounted for. The man Lei suspected was really behind the attacks, Terence Chang, still hadn't been identified doing anything but running a small, legitimate import-export business in Hilo. Rumor had it that he was the new head of the Chang crime empire, and business was booming—but even Ang's best FBI online tracing hadn't been able to identify a clear trail to that.

Sophie went on. "I think he's onto our taps. I suspect he's gone completely old-school, keeping everything off-line and maybe even using radios and pagers. You should talk to some of your old friends in Hilo PD when you're there. I also know, from that other case, that Chang has the skills to build a firewall I can't get through. Though more likely, he's masked himself behind multiple hidden identities."

"I have been in touch with Hilo PD, and they're still looking at him for drug dealing, prostitution, cockfighting, and gambling. You know what the new illegal gambling craze is over there?" Lei said.

"No, what?"

"Mah-jongg. They're opening these 'parlors' in houses. You can go to play and gamble. Someone's organizing it and getting a cut."

"Interesting. Well, thought you should know Marcella's on the Mainland, testifying on a case."

"How long is she going to be gone?"

"Up to a couple of weeks. You feeling okay?" Sophie asked, her brows drawn together.

"I'm feeling great, but I need to move on this soon, before getting around becomes too hard," Lei said. "Thanks for being my backup."

"What are you going to do?"

"Not sure yet. Just going to go over there for my other case and see what I can pick up on my own."

"I'll let you know if I find anything, but like I said, he's been quiet."

"Quiet like a snake. Talk soon." Lei cut the connection, frowning.

Lei glanced through the photos in the case jacket on the desk before her. She'd made a copy of the whole police file and smuggled it out of the station, suppressing guilt as she did so. It was her friend Pono's case, and he was dead-ended on it. She knew he wouldn't like her investigating Chang any more than Stevens would, but it was time to jump outside the box before she was too pregnant to have any options.

Lei looked at the file periodically to stay motivated, even though it was emotionally harrowing to do so. Sometimes looking at the material generated new ideas.

She came to the photo of her aunt. Aunty Rosario lay dead in her bed, her pallor waxen. A wire-wrapped C-4 bomb rested on her stomach and a shroud was puddled at her feet, where Lei had moved it from her aunt's face.

Could Anchara's killer, a foreign national, really have hired the killer that had left the bomb at her aunt's house? Could he have navigated this island on his own so well that he could find Anchara? Find and attack Stevens at their home?

It was highly unlikely that the man had acted alone. Someone with hacking skills must have provided him all the information he needed, but investigators hadn't been able to get the man to talk.

No, the shroud killer was just taking a break. Lulling them into complacency. And when they were most vulnerable, he'd strike again.

Lei's hand came to rest on the slight, hard roundness of her belly as she gazed at the terrible photos of Anchara's crime scene. By some miracle, Kiet had been uninjured.

No, the time to move was now. Lei couldn't lose her focus in the warm fuzziness of family life. The gambling case she was currently working was taking her to the Big Island anyway—it was the perfect cover.

Her fingers flew over the keyboard as she made reservations. She locked the shroud file in the small fireproof safe she'd told Stevens she kept work notes in. She'd bought another one for him, too, to keep him from being suspicious.

She couldn't ask Stevens to work with her on this. She already knew it wasn't his style to bend the rules, and he'd want to protect her or some such old-fashioned thing, especially now that she was pregnant. Right after their wedding, he'd promised he'd turn her in himself if he needed to protect her. Now that they had Kiet, Lei had a better idea of a baby's total vulnerability. And being pregnant just meant that she had that much more to protect.

It was time, maybe past time, to go on the offensive.

The Fireman frowned at his phone, holding up the small screen to reread the text he'd received. Enlisting your considerable fire skills to set a fire for a target I need eliminated. Cash deposit left in your mailbox to prove I'm serious.

Discovering that a man had died in that last fire had shocked him. He'd been unable to sleep last night, thinking about it, but this morning he was accepting it. The Bitch needed to be fed, and she ate whatever was in her path. He wasn't responsible that some homeless man sleeping off a bender in the fields got toasted for her pleasure.

His fascination with the Bitch had begun in his teens. He knew from the firebug forums he liked to visit that most people experimented with setting fires at some point in their childhood, but only a small percentage developed the love of fire he had. He'd been thrilled when his skills with fire had been called for at his job. It had all been perfect—until they'd laid him off.

More fool them.

The Fireman looked out the window of his apartment onto the row of dilapidated mailboxes in the parking lot. Fear hollowed his belly. How could he have been found? His number was unlisted, and from his avid news watching last night and his monitoring of the police band, no one was even close to discovering him.

He hoisted up jeans that were falling off his hips as he stood. He'd lost weight in the months since he was laid off. His apartment was a small one-bedroom in a tired old building in Wailuku, all he'd been able to afford after his savings ran out.

It wouldn't hurt to check the mailbox, just see what this was about.

He slid his feet into worn rubber slippers and clumped down the metal stairs on the exterior of the building, its tattered coconut palm in the corner of the parking lot. Hot midday sun beat down on the crown of his head as he opened the rusted mailbox.

Inside was a large, padded manila envelope with his name printed on it. Seeing his name in bold, block print made that empty, chilled feeling of fear tighten into something even stronger. He removed the envelope and glanced around. A car whizzed by on the road. Dazzling white clouds mocked him from the blue sky, and the cool green shadow of Iao Valley reached out to him—but otherwise, all was deserted in his seedy neighborhood.

The Fireman tucked the thick envelope under his arm and hurried back into the apartment. Sitting at his battered Formica table, he tore open the envelope, his hands trembling. He pulled too hard in his anxiety, and the package gave at the savage rip.

Hundred-dollar bills fluttered down around his feet like leaves in a fall wind.

He crouched, picking them up and piling them alongside the thick stack still left in the envelope. He sat down, knees quivering, and counted the bills.

Ten thousand in hundreds and a folded note in the same print. Got your attention? Put that stop sign you stole in the window, and I'll text you the address I want burned. When it's done, I'll drop another ten grand in your box and a five-thousand-dollar bonus for every human casualty.

"Someone out there is a loony tune," the Fireman muttered aloud.

He glanced around his barren apartment. The cigarette-burned lounger he'd picked up free from the curb faced an empty wall. He'd even had to sell his TV last month to pay rent. Twenty thousand, maybe more if there were "human casualties," would keep him for a year, if he was careful.

Besides, he didn't really have a choice. Whoever this was knew his identity. What he was. Where he lived. If he didn't do what they wanted, there was no reason not to rat him out—in fact, that threat was implicit in the bold way his name was printed on the envelope.

Moving slowly, the Fireman lifted the battered stop sign he'd stolen from one of his ignition sites into the window. How did this person know about the sign, even? Looking around, he realized the window was uncovered, and someone in a nearby building could probably see right in.

He closed the blind, lowering it down behind the stop sign and resolving to keep it down permanently. He sat back down and counted his money again. That comforting activity didn't stop his mouth from going dry as his phone dinged with an incoming text message containing an address.

Stevens and Ferreira, along with Tim Owen, ranged around the remains of the burn victim on the steel table in the morgue. The portly ME, bright in a rainbow-covered aloha shirt, pushed magnifying glasses onto the top of his head as he gestured to the body. "Cause of death is asphyxiation from smoke inhalation. Burns are secondary. Tox screens will take a couple of weeks, but the stomach was empty. I'm guessing he'll have a high blood-alcohol count."

"I've found the point of origin of the fire," the young investigator said. He spoke in the nasal voice of someone mouth breathing. The body's odor and appearance hadn't improved with the autopsy. Stevens peered closely at the victim's red, swollen and blistered face.

"We're interested in that, of course," Stevens said. "But we're more interested in who this man was. Did you find any ID? Anything on or near the body?"

"No," Dr. Gregory said. "Nothing in his pockets but a beer opener." He handed the scorched item, neatly bagged, to Stevens. "Wasn't enough skin left on his fingers to take prints. Maybe there's a print on the beer opener."

Stevens turned to Owen. "Did you find where this man was camping in the field? Maybe there was something left at his campsite."

"I did." Owen took out his file and opened it on an unoccupied steel table beside the body. They clustered around the fan of photos he spread out. "See this directionality?" He pointed to the way the sugarcane was pointing. "I could see which way the cane had burned from this and could see the remaining leaves on the downwind side. The char pattern is also rough in the direction of the point of origin. I found three spots along the cane-haul access road that tested positive for hydrocarbons, indicating a petroleum-based accelerant. I also found the remains of a gas can." Owen held up a photo of a blackened metal can with a blown-out crack in it, lying in a gridded area.

"This is what remains of a gas can that tested positive for the same residual trace as the origin sites."

"What does that mean?" Ferreira asked. Stevens saw the gleam of Vicks on the older detective's handlebar mustache below his nose, and he wished he'd thought of putting some on to head off the smell.

"It means the arsonist must have been careless. This can exploding would have been like a mine. No reason I can think of that he would have left it in the fire."

"Any fingerprints?" Stevens asked.

"Actually, I did get a partial. Kind of a miracle." Owen flipped to a blown-up photo of several whorls of a fingerprint, outlined in the black of char. "Lucky to have this. Brought an extra photo for you."

"Excellent." Stevens took the photo.

"So you said you found where this guy was camping?" Ferreira indicated the body on the table.

"Yes. He had a small tent. Must have been able to keep the spiders out that way." Owen gave a nod to Stevens. "The tent was burned, but I was able to find and identify the remains of the fabric, and the make is by Coleman." He showed them another photo. "See all these bottles? Looks like you were probably right, Dr. Gregory. This guy was holed up out there on a bender. Didn't find any ID, though."

They wrapped up the meeting, and Stevens and Ferreira walked out with Owen to go to the sugar mill headquarters. "Been out there yet?" Ferreira asked Owen as they reached their vehicles in the parking lot.

"Yeah, we've had a meeting already," Owen said, gesturing toward the central area of the island before he got into a bright yellow Maui Fire Department truck.

"I know right where the admin building is," Ferreira said to Stevens. Stevens handed his keys to Ferreira, and the burly older detective got behind the wheel of the Bronco.

"Let's take the lead on this interview," Stevens said as Ferreira fired up the vehicle. "Even though Owen set it up, this investigation's already out of his purview now that we know it's an arson homicide." Each state had a different way of investigating fire crime. In Hawaii, fire investigators focused exclusively on the causes of fire, and criminal investigation went to law enforcement.

"No argument there. Kid's wet behind the ears."

"Maybe, but he seems to know his stuff. Takes initiative, too." Stevens already felt a little protective of Tim Owen. He knew how hard it could be to get established in a place like Hawaii, with so many hidden social rules and agendas.

For some reason that reminded him of Anchara's simple life on Maui after their divorce. She'd been making a place here for herself and her son—before her life was stolen from her and her baby came to Stevens by default. Her murder would always haunt him.

He decided it always should.

They drove through the nondescript sprawl of urbanization that was downtown Kahului, but right outside of town, Ferreira turned left onto a semi-deserted one-lane asphalt road crusted with the red, iron-rich soil of the island. They drove down the narrow road bordered by tall, waving sugarcane and turned right into the mill area.

The rusted steel outbuildings and belching stacks of the processing plant rose around them like a factory out of a Dickens novel. Ferreira navigated past a row of parked red Ford trucks caked in filth and down an alley between towering corrugated metal buildings. A clattering rumble of machinery surrounded them and made it hard to think, and the cab of the truck filled with the rich, tactile scent of boiling molasses.

"I'm in favor of the sugar industry, but you wouldn't see me working here," Ferreira said, parking in front of a rusty metal outbuilding with no windows.

"It's quite a contrast to the beaches—that's for sure," Stevens said, stepping out of the truck into the parking lot. Dirt rose in reddish, powdery puffs under his boots.

Owen had parked beside them, and he got out of the yellow

truck. "Gonna have to wash this when I get back to base," he said, gesturing to the residue that already coated the vehicle.

"That's why the workers stay covered up." Ferreira pointed to a group of workers getting off a beat-up old school bus. They were attired in long-sleeved shirts and pants, big cloth hats, and bandannas covering their faces. "Let's get inside where it's air-conditioned."

Lei walked onto the plane and slid her tightly packed backpack into the overhead compartment. She took out the case file to review during the flight. Settling in her seat, she wrestled one last time with her conscience.

She should have at least called Stevens. She'd gotten better at remembering to communicate, but she didn't want to call now and have Stevens realize there was more going on than she was willing to say. Once she was in Hilo and checked into the cheap motel she'd picked out, she could text him. If he called, she'd tell him about the case that had brought her over to the Big Island. Less was more right now.

Still, Lei's gut roiled uneasily at the deception. "No help for it," she muttered.

How she was going to pull off anything useful remained to be seen.

She'd had to check her weapon in its special case, and she felt a little naked without it. She buckled her belt over her unfamiliarly tight waist and settled back in the seat, telling herself to relax.

She shut her eyes as the plane took off, remembering last night with a pang of guilty loss. After Lei locked everything back up in her office, she'd come out to the living room. Jared was gone. Kiet was asleep in his bouncy seat, an empty bottle beside him, and Stevens was on the couch.

"Alone at last." Stevens had hooked a long arm around Lei, hauling her over to him on the couch and giving her a thorough kiss. She'd melted against him, her tender breasts prickling with need. She didn't remember hearing about how pregnancy made women feel sexy, but now that the nausea was gone, Lei always seemed to be "in the mood." Just a look or a touch from her husband seemed to be enough to get her going these days.

Kiet belched softly from his seat.

"Well, not quite alone," Stevens said, turning back to the baby and loosening the straps that held him in. "I'll put him down. Meet you in the bedroom."

"I'll be a few minutes. Got to clean up." Lei went into the kitchen as he carried the baby off. She put away the leftovers and loaded the dishwasher. Part of their agreement with her dad was that he got a clean kitchen in the morning. She went to the bedroom after brushing her teeth, stepping inside and shutting the door.

He'd closed the curtains, and the light was off. In the total darkness, the known became new again. "Where are you?"

"Come into my parlor, said the spider to the fly." Stevens growled, and she smiled, feeling her way forward.

"Thought that was my line," Lei said. "I don't want to grab Keiki by mistake." The big Rottie slept on the bed with them.

"She's banished for the moment."

"Oh. You have some devious plan, I can tell."

"You told me you liked my devious plans. Back when we weren't old married folk."

"I do like your plans."

"No more talking."

Lei's heart rate spiked at his low, commanding tone. Her nipples tightened as a soft ache tugged at her. Prickling awareness rippled up her arms and made the tiny hairs rise in instant response.

She'd reached the side of the bed. As her eyes adjusted, she saw the faintest outline of his long, naked body, and her mouth went dry. She swallowed, trying to see more, savoring the anticipation. There was only enough light to glimpse the heavy curve of his shoulder, the slant of his side, the long plane of his extended thigh.

"Come here." His voice was a vibrating chord that thrilled her.

No, marriage and family hadn't quenched their passion. At least not yet.

Lei forced her attention back to the file, feeling bad again for leaving him. Deceiving him. Well, maybe nothing would come of it. She'd work her case and go home. Still, this was an opportunity to get an eye on the Changs' operation. She had to take it.

Fortunately, no one had taken the seat beside her, so she was able to open the file and sort through the records she'd collected on the gambling ring that had emerged on Maui. Just a week ago, a confidential informant she'd cultivated had gotten her involved in what was developing into a case with deep roots.

"So, mah-jongg one Chinese game," her CI, Claudine Figueroa, an innkeeper in Wailuku she'd met on a murder investigation, had told her. "I been getting these invitations on e-mail. Me and my friends, we like go. Sometimes we watch the players. Sometimes we play and we bet."

"How high are the stakes? I mean, this sounds like small potatoes," Lei said. She'd responded to Claudine's phone call that she had some "important information for the MPD," and now that she was here, at the woman's inn, the equivalent of organized bingo didn't sound like a big concern.

"Stakes are big. My second cousin, he lost his house in one of these games. Not only that, they get some boys breaking legs if people don't pay," Claudine said, sucking her dentures the way she did when upset. She plucked at the neck of a banana-yellow muumuu, and Lei spotted matching Crocs peeking out from underneath the hem.

"I can tell there's more going on than you're telling me." Lei fiddled with the rough, white-gold pendant she always wore.

"Those boys, they've already got us paying protection money," Claudine hissed, leaning forward to catch Lei's eye. "If it's not mah-jongg, it's blackjack or the lottery in the Mainland. They got an idea for everyone who like gamble, and you don't get hooked on something, they keep trying until you do."

"Protection money? And who is 'they'?"

"I don't know exactly. Six months ago, these two guys, they

came around to all the small-kine businesses in Wailuku. Nobody knows them, but they're big guys, armed. They tell us they charging one 'tax' for keep doing business here. Some of us no like pay the tax. And you remember the building wen' burn down on Market Street? That guy, he no like pay." Claudine's pidgin thickened with her agitation. "I tell the husband, we going pay. So we do. Then next thing, we getting e-mails about all the things they like us to gamble on."

"Why didn't you tell me sooner?" Lei asked. "When you had that homicide at your inn? It might have been important."

"No, I nevah like deal with it then. Now I know this just going get worse and worse until they bleed us dry, and it's got to stop. After my cuz lost his house, I say enough already. And I know you. That's why I call you. You one good girl."

Lei smiled at that description. "I have to take this back to the station and see if my captain wants to assign it to Vice. I usually work Homicide. But thanks for the tip, Claudine. I'll get back to you no matter what."

Captain Omura had ended up authorizing Lei to run with the case. Lei was working it alone because she was currently without a partner, due to resigning from the hazardous explosives detail. Abe Torufu, her partner on that assignment, was now training with another detective who'd volunteered to take her place on the bomb squad.

And it was just as well she didn't have a partner, Lei thought, as she leafed through her notes. Through interviews, she'd uncovered persistent rumors that both the "protection" payments and organized gambling had their roots in the Changs' Big Island operation and that the two thugs who collected payment were unknown to Maui folks because they came over from that island. Last week, when she'd asked to go to Hawaii to check out the situation, Omura had given the okay.

But Omura didn't know Lei had been ordered by the FBI not to have anything further to do with any investigation involving the

Changs. Lei would have been perfectly happy to honor that if she didn't suspect Terence Chang had somehow found a way to kill Anchara and her aunt and set Stevens up for murder.

And Chang was still holding on to one more shroud.

She shut the folder, reclined her seat, and closed her eyes for the short flight. Her mind immediately went back to the bedroom with Stevens. The remnants of that rich memory didn't make it easier to get off the plane, knowing she was going after their enemy behind his back instead of by his side.

CHAPTER FOUR

THE FIREMAN DID a preliminary assessment of the address he'd received, and the results were daunting. As he drove back toward Kahului, he mulled over the challenges. On the plus side, it was a remote location that he could probably approach relatively undetected. Potential fuel in the form of tall eucalyptus robusta trees surrounded the property. The trees, while green, had a lot of combustible sap. The house itself was also highly flammable, an old wooden structure on a post-and-pier foundation with a tin roof, which, if properly ignited, could go up fast and deadly.

On the minus side, the house was surrounded by a ten-foot cedar fence and appeared to have a security system, not something he'd been prepared to breach. According to the TMK map he pulled up, inside the fence were two dwellings: a cottage close to the fence and a main house with thirty feet of open lawn that would provide a firebreak. He pulled the truck over and hiked back through the vacant lot bordering the property to get a look inside. Climbing a tree, he was able to look over the fence into the yard, and that's when he spotted the Rottweiler.

It had spotted him, too, and the deep bellow of its bark shriveled his balls. He'd almost fallen getting out the tree.

He hated dogs of any kind. Guard dogs aroused even more antipathy. Twenty thousand wasn't looking like good or easy money anymore. He wanted more if he was going to figure out how to navigate these multiple challenges.

Back at his apartment, he took out his phone and texted the number he'd received the original message from: Challenges with assignment. Dog. Fence. Security system. Firebreaks. Green trees. Need more money for this job.

He waited. No reply.

"Asshole," the Fireman muttered. He had only one real way to communicate.

He got up and set the stop sign in the window. The blinds remained down behind the sign, as he'd left them since he'd figured out how he was being observed, and now his already-depressing apartment was always semi-gloomy except for the new flat screen he'd bought the day the money arrived.

Even if he didn't hear back, he needed to get a fire plan. Sitting down with a pencil and paper, he copied the TMK map of the property and planned his assault. When he was done with that, he made a list of materials he could use for the ignition.

Imagining every stage of setting fire to the challenging fortress of a property energized him, and even though his phone remained stubbornly silent, his spirits lifted.

He was the Fireman. He could do this. If he could just get into the house, he could set a fire that would be a masterpiece of destruction.

Stevens and Owen followed Ferreira through a metal-faced door into the administration offices of the sugarcane company. Inside a linoleum foyer area with a heavy rubber mat stood a wooden shoe rack where various boots were lined up. Ferreira called to the receptionist on the other side of a half wall.

"Cheryl! How you stay?"

"Keeping cool," the middle-aged woman said. Her black hair was scraped into a bun and her cheeks were acne-scarred. "What you here for, cuz?"

"Meeting with the brass. Got us on the calendar?"

"Yes, I see you right here. Welcome to Maui Sugar," Cheryl said, including Stevens and Owen with a gracious nod. "Can you gentlemen please put your boots on the rack? As you can see, we have a little dirt situation around here. I'll show you to the conference room."

"No problem." Owen sat beside Stevens on a conveniently located chair and undid his laces. Stevens did likewise, darting an assessing glance around the utilitarian space, a room built into the prefabricated metal building using studs and drywall. In their socks, the men followed Cheryl's ample rear down the hall. She opened a door and gestured them into a conference room surrounded in whiteboards. A wheezing AC unit was set flush in the windowless wall. "Can I get you anything to drink? Tea? Coffee?"

"I'd love some coffee," Stevens said. "Black is fine."

"Water for me," said Owen.

"Nothing, thanks," Ferreira said. "But is the restroom still down the hall?"

"Sure is." Cheryl led Ferreira out, and Owen and Stevens sat down at the Formica conference table.

"Never took a meeting in my socks before," Owen said.

"Get used to it," Stevens responded. "Cultural thing. Though in this building, I think it's just that they want to keep the dirt on the mat in front."

Ferreira reappeared. "I wanted to get my cousin alone for a few minutes, to see what she might have picked up about the fires. She had a few names she thought were good to investigate, guys who'd been fired or laid off and had an attitude about it. We can see if they jibe with the ones the administration offers up."

As if on cue, the door opened on two men in business casual. Ferreira stood first, shaking the taller one's hand. "Hey, Jake."

"Josh Ferreira! Didn't expect you here; thought we were talking to the fire investigator." The stocky man with thinning hair glanced around, and Tim Owen popped up, extending his hand.

"And we've met before. Hi again. Tim Owen, fire investigator for Maui County."

"Jake Schumacher. I'm the general manager. This is Fred Okasako, director of operations." Stevens introduced himself, and they all sat back down after the obligatory small talk about where everyone was from.

Stevens glanced at Tim Owen, and the young man caught his eye, clearing his throat to get everyone's attention.

"I asked for this meeting to discuss the series of arson cane fires you've been experiencing in Maui Sugar fields. For the benefit of the detectives here, I'll just recap that we have met twice before, discussing various aspects of these fires. I've given the management here some ideas regarding prevention, which we should discuss again. But now that there's been a fatality, the criminal aspect of the investigation is going to shift to the Maui Police Department. I will continue to work closely with the detectives to investigate any fire-related aspects of the case."

"Thanks for clarifying the roles and responsibilities," Okasako said. He was shorter and stockier than Schumacher, but he carried himself with the solid authority of a leader. "Jake is the 'big kahuna' in charge of all aspects of the Maui Sugar operation; my responsibility is operations, in which I oversee personnel and human resources as one aspect. We have more than eight hundred employees working in various capacities."

"Didn't realize you had so many," Stevens said, leaning forward to make contact with the man he sensed was the real head of the company. "We want to focus on any employees who might be disgruntled and possibly have fire-setting experience from working with your controlled-harvesting burns."

"Tim had given us a heads-up about that. I was talking with my department heads and we prepared a list." Okasako produced a type-written set of names with addresses and phone numbers. "Some of these are current employees. Some were laid off a few months ago during budget cuts—as you may have heard, we aren't making much of a profit these days—and some were fired for cause."

Stevens took the paper and scanned down it. "I see you have fifty names here. That's going to be tough. Do you have some you'd prioritize?"

Okasako met Stevens's eye with his own direct, pebble-hard gaze. "I'd start with the ones who were fired, then the ones who were laid off."

Jake Schumacher leaned forward. "What we noticed is that the fields being burned were close to harvest. By burning them a couple of weeks before harvest, there's been an attempt to ruin our harvest, which implies a financial revenge motive. At least from our perspective. What we haven't shared publicly is that this arsonist isn't really hurting us that badly. Yeah, we've lost some tonnage, but we've still been able to harvest and process a good deal of what he's burned."

"Do you think he knows this?" Stevens asked, tapping the paper with his finger.

"We've kept it out of the news for this reason. Talked to the reporter and asked her to exaggerate the damage," Schumacher said. "We don't want him to start burning the one-year cane. That would really put us back."

Stevens narrowed his eyes. "From here on out, we need to be informed and a part of any information that is circulating to the public. So you refer to the arsonist as 'he.' Any particular reason?"

"Most of our burn and harvest crews are male," Okasako said.

"And most arsonists, statistically speaking, are male," Owen interjected.

"So who knows which fields you're going to burn?" Stevens asked. "Seems like this perp has some insider knowledge."

"Actually, that's a matter of public record. Right on our website," Schumacher said. "Because our burns affect the public in terms of health and safety, we have to post our burn schedule. It's right there on our website year-round, and we mail out letters to neighborhoods affected a couple weeks ahead of time."

"What about protests about your controlled burns?" Stevens asked. "I've seen some very vocal people complaining about air-quality concerns and so forth related to the harvesting. Have you received any hate mail or other targeted complaints?"

Beside him, he could see Ferreira shaking his head, but Okasako nodded. "I already thought of that. I've had our administrative assistants set aside any threatening or otherwise negative correspondence." He reached into the file folder he'd walked in with and took out a rubber-banded stack of letters. "These range from scientific articles linking the cane smoke to cancer and asthma to rants about bringing down property values."

"Thank you." Stevens took the letters. "It was an idea of mine that, besides sour-grapes-employee concerns, these fires could be about drawing attention to the burn debate."

"There's no debate," Schumacher snapped. "Burning is the most efficient method of harvest. Period."

"What about those turbine-style harvesters I've seen used beside the major highways, where there's a safety concern with traffic?"

"Expensive. And if you consider the carbon footprint generated by the gas the turbines burn, it's not that much better."

Stevens frowned. "I'd love to see some statistics on that and a fuller discussion on why machine harvesters aren't an option—or at least on why some people think they should be. Might speak to motive."

"We won't settle that issue here," Okasako snapped. "Let's stay focused on our mutual interest in solving this case."

"That's what we're here for. Solving the crime that's affecting your operations," Ferreira said from beside Stevens. Stevens felt his hackles rise at his subordinate's conciliatory tone.

"More important, solving a murder case. A man has lost his life." Stevens bit off his words.

"A homeless man, camping in our fields," Schumacher said dismissively.

"A human being," Stevens said. "Who died in excruciating pain." He opened his own file and pushed a couple of photos of the "human chicken wing" over to the two Maui Sugar employees. Schumacher paled, but Okasako took a long look. He raised his eyes to Stevens's, expression unchanged.

"We are in no way responsible for this man's death," Okasako said. "And we want to make sure this not only doesn't happen again, but that the person who set the fire is prosecuted to the full extent of the law."

Stevens put the pictures back into the file. "Good. Then we're all on the same page. Anybody have any ideas about motive other than what we've explored?"

Schumacher nodded. "A lot of people have said they thought it might just be kids causing trouble. Thinking fire-setting is fun and won't hurt anybody."

Tim Owen spoke up. "There are a few reasons I don't think it's kids. The accelerant used to start the fires, for one, is a mix of two-thirds diesel and one-third gasoline. The gasoline combusts upon ignition, catching the diesel, which clings to the fuel source, helping the burn really take hold. While it's possible it's a kid who's done a little homework to know that, more likely it's an adult with some knowledge of fire science."

"Well, the public seems to keep putting that teen theory forth. I wonder if you have a list of employees with teenagers?" Ferreira asked.

Okasako inclined his head. "Might take HR a little while, but I can pull together a list for you."

"That reminds me—we were going to discuss the safety recommendations I suggested," Owen said. "Why don't I revisit them for the group?"

Schumacher nodded.

"Okay." Owen took out a paper. "I believe I gave this to you after the first two fires. First: Increase company security patrols around your harvest-ready fields."

"We've done that as best we can with our personnel challenges," Okasako said.

"Second: Take down the postings about the burn schedule to obscure the targets more."

"We can't. Part of our agreement with the county is that the burn schedule is made public," Schumacher said.

"I still think you could technically fulfill that requirement while making the information less accessible," Owen argued. "But we can discuss later. Next: Install surveillance cams on the power poles in the field. That might help catch the arsonist on video."

"We're looking into that," Okasako said. "So far the bids we've received are prohibitively expensive."

"All right. That's your choice as a company." Owen looked down at his list, and Stevens felt his estimation of the young man rising. Tim Owen was being authoritative, making sure the company couldn't shift blame to him and the fire department if the fires continued. "Make firebreaks using the turbine harvesters right after you stop watering to contain the size of the fires."

"We plan to do that. We can afford to cut the fields up into smaller grids using the harvesters and burn them in sections," Okasako said.

"Good. Here's another one: Lock the cane-haul road gates and restrict the key access. I've observed that your gates are usually open, and people are using your roads as informal shortcuts. You could easily stop the traffic."

"Yes. I thought that was already done." Schumacher looked at Okasako.

Okasako shook his head. "Everyone was complaining so much I lifted the restriction, but I'll get the foremen locking all the gates again. It's a hassle for our employees, but the ones who need access can all get keys."

"It's just while you're under fire, as it were," Owen said. "Once we catch this perpetrator, things can be more relaxed. Tell them that when they grumble. Okay, just one more. Install outdoor smoke alarms along your access roads. This could help warn anyone camping or hiding in the fields that the cane is on fire."

"That's pretty easy. We can do that," Okasako said. "We'll see if it doesn't just drive everyone nuts going off at the wrong kinds of smoke."

"That's all I've got right now," Owen said.

Stevens stood. "I think we have a good start here. We'll be in touch with anything further. Give us a call if you hear anything, no matter how insignificant." He handed over cards to both managers. "Thanks for your help."

"We want to catch this guy more than you do," Schumacher said. Walking down the hall, Stevens wondered if that was really true. Based on their lukewarm implementation of Owen's suggestions, it didn't seem like it.

The Coconut Sunseeker was an old three-story building covered with lumpy spray-on exterior spackle. Its turquoise paint was grayish with Hilo's ever-present mildew. One of Hilo's gigantic spreading banyan trees hung over it, casting the motel into shade and rendering the name literal.

Lei set up her laptop on the rickety desk in her room. She'd paid cash and registered under a fake name, squelching the last dregs of guilt. She'd made a choice, chosen a path. Being off the radar was a necessary part of it, because she didn't know where this would lead. Stevens's words to her on the side of Haleakala right after their wedding rang in her ears: "I'll take you down myself if I have to, to keep you out of danger."

No, she couldn't tell him what she was doing, but he'd forgive her when she'd removed the threat. He always had before.

She called South Hilo Station, setting up interviews with her first commanding officer on the force, Captain Ohale, and his vice detectives. First order of business was to legitimize the trip.

She sent a text message to Stevens:

Phone is on the fritz. Had to go to Big Island for a gambling case. I'm buying a burner and will call you later—Omura has details if you need them. Don't worry. I love you and kisses to the little man!

Her heart actually ached, a tightness in her chest that shortened her breath, as she put this part in motion. She turned off the smartphone and removed the battery, then opened a cheap burner phone she'd picked up at Hilo's Longs.

She texted Stevens again, knowing that if he didn't have her number, he'd immediately suspect something—hell, he was going to suspect something anyway, just because she was on the Big Island—but she needed time.

Time to investigate her real gambling case.

Time to find Chang and see what he was up to.

And time to establish an alibi.

CHAPTER FIVE

STEVENS AND FERREIRA sat on either side of his desk back at Haiku Station with the list of names from Maui Sugar. Between families with teens, disgruntled employees, and complaint letters, it was quite a stack to work through. "How do you want to divide this up, boss?" Ferreira asked.

"Let's just cut it in half and then work the phones," Stevens said. "Let's start with running background checks on all of the employees. Then, if we get a ping off anything, someone with suspicious priors, we can put together a list of visits and interviews. I think we should go find them, get the element of surprise versus calling them to come in for interviews."

"Sounds good." Ferreira grabbed a pair of scissors and cut the list of employees in half, handing part to Stevens. "Done."

Stevens felt his mouth tug up in a smile, but he wanted to clear something up from the earlier interview.

"Joshua, I know you feel strongly about the cane company's right to keep doing what they've been doing, but we need to be able to follow every lead, even if it steps on toes."

"I thought we were playing 'good cop, bad cop' in that interview," Ferreira said, his expression neutral. "I want to keep playing 'good cop' to Maui Sugar, because as you saw, I'm related to a lot of people there and have a lot of friends there. But if you're asking where my loyalty lies, you should know me better than that."

"I just want to be sure," Stevens said. "We could end up finding out they're setting the fires themselves, for an insurance claim or something. You never know where the evidence will lead."

"Not likely on the insurance, since they were able to recoup most of the cane that was burned," Ferreira said. "But yeah. We'll follow wherever the evidence goes. Now, if you'll excuse me, got some background checks to run."

Stevens watched the older man depart, noting the stiffness in Ferreira's barrel-like posture and the red on the back of the man's weathered neck.

He'd offended Ferreira.

Stevens got up and shut his glass-windowed office door. He wasn't going to apologize. He needed his men to know he'd call them on contradictions. Ferreira had never given him any reason to wonder about his loyalty, and yet even in the face of Ferreira's support during his own investigation a few months ago, Stevens still found it hard to trust the other man.

Maybe it was because he'd been betrayed by a partner in Hilo before, in the worst possible way. He wished he could forget the man he'd worked with who'd tried to kill Lei. He never would. He lived with the scars on his wife every day. Ferreira was the closest thing he'd had to a partner since, because he'd refused to work with one after the Big Island.

As if he'd conjured his wife in his thoughts, his phone dinged with an incoming message from her. His brows knit, reading it. *Phone is on the fritz. Had to go to Big Island for a gambling case. I've bought a burner and will call you later—Omura has details if you need them. Don't worry. I love you, and kisses to the little man!*

On the Big Island? Why hadn't she said something last night?

He texted her back asking that very thing. Seconds later a ping back informed him that the message was undeliverable.

Phone on the fritz? How likely was that? He needed more information.

He grabbed the desk phone, speed-dialing Captain Omura's private line.

"Lieutenant Stevens." Omura's chilly tone doused his ire somewhat. The captain hated unprofessionalism and emotionality, not to mention lack of teamwork and communication, which this call would reveal. Stevens slowed his breathing with an effort, curling one hand into a fist so hard it hurt. The tiny purple heart with lei on it bulged on his tight forearm muscle. He put the phone between his ear and shoulder and rubbed the tattoo—hard—until it burned, as if he could erase it from his skin.

"Captain, I'm calling about Lei's trip to the Big Island."

"Yes." As usual, he heard the tapping of her keyboard. She didn't elaborate, making him ask what he wanted to know. Even as he was forced to do so, he admired her technique.

"I'm just checking that you authorized the trip."

"Yes. Couple of days. She's working a vice case." A pause, then the jab. It hurt even when he was braced for it. "Thought communication was a big part of marriage."

"You know Lei." He gritted his teeth.

"I know she's an excellent detective. Bit of a risk taker and one to cut corners, but she's on a mellow vice case." Omura's annoyance came through loud and clear. "I authorized three days, if that helps."

"Thank you. It does." He hung up with a bang and surged to his feet. A "mellow" vice case? The hairs on the back of his neck rose. Would she go after Terence Chang alone? No. She wouldn't be so crazy.

Adrenaline flooded his system in a hot jolt of rage born of fear and frustration. Her case had to have ties back to the Changs. Gambling was their main thing after drugs.

"Sonofabitch." He tried Lei's phone again, and it pinged back again.

He walked back and forth, trying to burn off the adrenaline while he called South Hilo Station, where he and Lei had first met. Lei wasn't the only one with connections there.

"Captain Ohale. This is Lieutenant Stevens on Maui."

"Mike! Speaking to you both in one day, what a pleasure. How's married life treating you?"

Stevens let out his breath in a whoosh. "You heard from Lei?"

"Yeah. She's in town for an investigation, coming in to talk with me about a case."

"What's it about?"

"Why are you asking?" Ohale's bass voice had gone slow. "Don't tell me she took off without telling you what she was doing."

"Nah." He didn't want to throw Lei under the bus with her old boss, so he tried for nonchalance. "I was just wondering if this had anything to do with the Changs. We're supposed to stay a long way away from them—orders to Lei from the FBI. She still has a liaison role with them. Thought you might want a heads-up."

"You saying you don't trust her to do that? Yeah, I guess we both know the answer to that." Stevens heard the creak of Ohale's old office chair as he leaned back. He could easily imagine the burly station chief pushing his tiny steel-rimmed readers onto the top of his head as he rubbed his eyes. "So married life hasn't settled her down yet?"

"It's fine," Stevens said, pinching the bridge of his nose. He didn't want to get into it.

"Well, she just told me she was here on a vice case, wanted to speak to my detectives. So I guess I'll find out more when we meet."

"Great. Just thought you should have a heads-up about the Chang thing. This came down to us from the FBI after that bust at the Chang compound a few years ago."

"I'll take it under advisement," Ohale said, and Stevens thanked him and hung up.

If Lei was investigating the Changs, he'd just thrown a major spoke in her wheel. He felt shitty about it—but it was for her own good and for the good of their unborn baby. He just didn't trust her. He felt bad about it, but it was the truth.

And anger boiled up again as his phone dinged with a text from an unknown number. *Here's my burner phone number so you don't worry. Lei.*

"Too late, Sweets," he said through gritted teeth, and called the number. "I'm onto you."

The new number rang and rang mockingly and then went to an inactivated voice mail box.

"Sonofabitch!" Stevens growled. He resisted the urge to throw his phone. Instead, he set it down carefully on the desk and thought through his options.

THE FIREMAN BOUGHT supplies at several different stores and paid in cash. Didn't use one of those stupid discount cards either. All those seemingly innocuous things, done for convenience, combined to create trails that could lead to him. He checked his phone for the hundredth time—and this time there was a text message.

No more money. Tech support will be arriving in the mail.

Tech support. What the hell could that be?

Back at his place, he gathered the materials together, along with a big black plastic container he could close and carry to the truck, hiding its contents. He lived in an apartment. There was no telling how many people were watching.

He stowed a battery-operated, handheld drill with a large-bore bit in the container, then poured a couple of gallons of his favorite mixture of gas and diesel fuel into a series of one-gallon Ziploc bags, sealing them double-tight to prevent leakage and smells that could alert anyone to a problem. He added a Christmas tree timer with a plug to the box and then took out a long orange extension cord.

Using a sharp paring knife, he cut the receptacle end off and peeled the plastic coating off the wires, exposing a couple inches of wire, which he then crossed carefully. A bottle of nail polish remover and big bag of cotton balls completed his preparations.

But none of it was going anywhere if he couldn't get access to the house.

He'd have to wait for that "tech support" and see how the black-mailer could help him breach the house's security measures.

The Fireman had bought a barbecue starter as part of his supplies. He almost flicked it on, just to see the narrow tongue of flame come out of the metal wand and dance for him a little, but he remembered that gas fumes were still trapped in his living space. There might be enough to combust.

He opened all the windows, turned on the fan, and checked that the gas can was screwed shut tight, that the Ziploc bags were sealed and stowed in the plastic container. When he was sure the apartment was clear, he lay down on the couch and flicked the lighter on, watching the steady glow of the flame, passing his hand through it just to feel its hot kiss. He'd write a post for his online Fireman Journal. *Kissing the flame.* It was a safe enough topic.

And mentally, he planned every step of the ignition.

LEI WALKED through the worn doors of South Hilo Station with a sense of déjà vu. The watch officer behind the desk was unfamiliar, though, and she had to show ID and sign the logbook. After that, though, it was a slow route across the bullpen as she stopped by various desks to greet old friends on her way to Captain Ohale's office.

Finally reaching her destination, Lei smoothed her hair back off her forehead and adjusted her tight waistband as she faced the blank wooden door with the tiny brass plaque that said Captain Ohale on it.

She lifted her hand and knocked.

Almost immediately the door opened. From his casual clothing, she could tell that the man holding the door open for her was a detective. "Welcome to Hilo, Sergeant Texeira," he said. "I'm Jed Campos."

She shook his hand. "Thanks! Lei Texeira."

Ohale stood up behind his desk. "Lei! Great to see you on the old stomping grounds!"

Another detective was seated in the other chair in front of the captain's desk, and he also rose. She met Detective Sam Kilohana, as well, and greeted her old captain with a hug. "Great to see you, too, sir."

"Well, I hear you're a mama now," Ohale said.

Lei knew he was referring to Kiet and she nodded. "It's a big adjustment, but Kiet's an easy baby. Which, of course, means I want to wrap this case up as soon as I can and get home to him." She didn't mention the baby on the way. He might have heard about it, but here in a male-dominated work environment, wasn't the place to mention it.

They sat down, and Lei told them about her confidential informant's comments about the knee-breakers from the Big Island. "Have you heard anything about organized online gambling with mah-jongg, or other gambling games?"

Campos had a pointed goatee on his chin, and he stroked it thoughtfully. "I've heard a rumor about this, but we didn't follow up. Didn't know it was originating in this area, and with cockfighting, dogfighting, and plenty of other things to track down, it seemed pretty small—*manini*."

"That's what I thought, too, until my CI told me the stakes were high—her cousin lost his house in one of the games. She said the same organization sending 'tax enforcers' over to Maui is the one soliciting them to participate in gambling activities."

"How do they know that?" Ohale asked, rubbing his reading glasses with a big red bandanna.

"She told me some of the other business owners decided to follow the men. They tracked them to the airport, where they took a flight to the Big Island."

"Still." Campos frowned. "Civilians tracking these guys, really?"

"Someone's got a cousin who works the desk at Hawaiian Airlines," Lei said with a smile. "As how they know for sure."

"As always how," Kilohana said, with a wry grin. "Hawaiian-style detecting."

"Seriously, though, these folks are spooked. My CI said one of the owners refused to pay, and the next week his business burned down."

"That is serious," Campos said. "But how are you connecting that with us in South Hilo?"

This was the tricky part, Lei knew. She had to move ahead with her case and still conceal her real agenda. She shrugged and sat back in her chair. "Thought I'd start somewhere where I knew the players."

"You mean us at South Hilo PD or the Chang crime family?" Ohale asked, his dark eyes unreadable. "Had a call from Lieutenant Stevens on Maui. He had some concerns about the Changs."

"I can imagine," Lei said, keeping her expression neutral even as her stomach clenched in response to this news—Stevens was checking up on her. She expected it, but the evidence that he didn't trust her still hurt. "They keep turning up like a bad penny, behind sex trafficking, gambling, money laundering, and a couple of attempts on our lives."

The two detectives glanced at each other, clearly confused, but Ohale kept his eyes on Lei. "So is there a connection that you know of between this case and the Changs?"

"No. I just came to you to see what you folks might know about this situation on Maui, and talking to you was a place to start," Lei said. She felt a queasy roll in her gut, like the early morning sickness days, followed by something that felt like a flutter against the tightness of her jeans waistband. What a strange feeling—she probably had gas and was about to embarrass herself. She put her hands in her lap and unobtrusively pressed, willing the problem to go away before she had to run to the bathroom.

"Well, the Changs often come up as suspects. In fact, the FBI has requested we keep the compound in upper Hilo under regular surveillance. I think they may even have some wire taps on Terence Chang since his grandma died," Ohale said. "But there's been nothing. From what we can tell, Terence Chang is running a totally legit import-export business, most of it done online."

"Huh," Lei said. This was what she'd expected to hear about Chang, but she didn't believe it. And even with her hands pressed on her abdomen, she felt the strange fluttering sensation again. Could it be the baby kicking? She'd read that could be felt as early as four months. She felt her cheeks flush as it happened again, and a buoyant feeling of exultation suffused her.

Their baby was really there, growing, making itself known, right here in a meeting. She wished she could call Stevens right this minute and tell him.

"What's wrong?" Captain Ohale's sharp eyes had never left her face, and though she'd gotten better at concealing her thoughts and feelings, Stevens could always read her like a book, and so could her old boss.

"Nothing," Lei said, scrambling. "I have a lead I'd like to follow up on, a place to start at least. My CI forwarded me a photo of the guys who are collecting the 'tax' on Maui. I wonder if we could do some facial recognition with your database. I didn't have time to run that on Maui."

"Sure," Campos said. "Why don't Kilohana and I pull up all we have on the organized gambling? And you can go to the computer lab and work on that. Captain tells us you'll remember the way there, from your days here."

"Sounds like a plan," Lei said with a smile. "I'll find you at your office when I'm done."

The detectives got up to leave, and Lei made a motion to follow.

"Stay a minute," Ohale said. It wasn't a request. Lei sat back down, her hands still resting protectively on her waist. Kilohana shut the captain's glass-inset door behind him, leaving Lei with Ohale.

Her old boss leaned forward, steepling his fingers. "Tell me about what's going on with you and the Changs."

Lei shrugged. "Old business. I always think something's up with them."

"Not good enough. Stevens was very specific. He told me you were ordered by the FBI not to have anything to do with them. I was involved from start to finish in that bust with Terence Chang when you were in the FBI, but somehow I never got the memo on that, and I don't appreciate it." His voice had risen. "So if you're here on some trumped-up fishing expedition against your old enemies and using my office as a cover, that's not going to fly."

The accuracy of Ohale's conclusion chilled Lei, and she knew she needed to dispel it. Instead, she decided more truth was in order. If he found out her situation later, from someone else, trust would be lost in this valuable relationship.

"I'm sorry, sir. I never thought something would come up with them again. I thought we were done with the Changs after Healani's death, but then we started getting threats. They escalated." Lei told him about the shrouds and the more recent deaths of those close to her associated with them. "We have the perp in custody—or I should say, he's been deported—but we don't know anyone who could be after us like this other than the Changs. They've made it personal."

"How do you know that? Do you have even one shred of evidence?"

"No, but listen to this." Lei told him about the attack on Stevens and about Kiet's mother's murder. "It's hard for Stevens and me to believe that this guy, a foreign national, could have navigated the US and even found our address without inside help. Accurate outside help. And I know Terence Chang is an expert with computers."

"So you don't have anything tying the shrouds—and that killer—to the Chang family."

Lei frowned. "Not specifically. But who else?"

"Well, you've had a directive, and I'm enforcing it. No contact or messing with the Changs. Trust me when I tell you we're all over

Terence Chang like white on rice. So no make trouble over here, like you always doing." He'd lapsed into pidgin in his agitation. "Do your job, and go home to your family."

Lei felt her cheeks flush again. "Like a good little mama, you mean? Screw that. This shroud killer is going after my family, and I'm going to stop it."

"Not in my backyard, Lei Texeira. Not on my watch. Let others handle this one. That's an order."

Lei stood up, balling her fists. "You're not my commanding officer anymore. Sir."

"No, but you're in my dog patch now, and Omura's a phone call away. Don't think I won't have her yank you out of here faster than you can turn around. So keep your nose clean, do your investigation with my boys, and go home in one piece. This is the last time I warn you."

Lei narrowed her eyes, feeling angry heat flash over her, but she held herself still and let out her breath slowly. It would never do to aggravate her old boss. He could indeed get her yanked out of there, and with a police escort back to the airport. No doubt that was what Stevens was hoping. A new wave of anger, this time at her husband, flashed through her body.

"Thanks for the warning, sir, but I assure you it's not necessary. I may be worried about the Changs, but I'd be crazy to go after any of them alone and without probable cause," Lei said when she was sure her voice and demeanor were under control. "Thanks for the support from Vice. I'll check back if we find a connection to my case on Maui."

Ohale sat back, avuncular and friendly again. "Glad we understand each other, then. So what's going on with your stomach? You feeling okay?"

Her former chief was an observant man. Lei dropped her hands from where they still covered her waist, a dead giveaway. She decided to tell Ohale—it would be obvious soon anyway. "Actually, I'm pregnant."

"Congratulations!" Ohale's face broke into a huge grin. "Caprice is going to be thrilled to hear this!"

Caprice. Dr. Wilson, Lei's former therapist. Lei felt her smile freeze—Dr. Wilson was going to hear she was in town and want to see her now. She'd forgotten Ohale and Dr. Wilson were dating. "Yeah, we were waiting to tell anyone until it was for sure, but I'm about four months along."

"Well, hell, girl, you should have said so in the first place."

"Wasn't the time to bring it up in front of the guys."

"Telling me would have saved you that lecture about the Changs."

"Why?" Lei felt angry heat brush the back of her neck again. "Because I'm pregnant, I wouldn't go after the Changs?"

Ohale narrowed his eyes. "Of course. You'd know better than to do a damn-fool thing like that with another life at stake."

Lei felt paralyzed, hearing it put that way. Her justifications for what she'd been planning began to crumble. This really was putting more than just herself at risk, and with the fluttering of kicks underneath her waistband, it was hard to ignore that other life.

But the hell of it was, the baby was at risk anyway, with the shroud killer still out there. They all were.

CHAPTER SIX

Stevens worked his way steadily through his half of the list of employees at Maui Sugar, checking their records. He began with those fired or laid off in the last year. Three had old drug charges, several had misdemeanors, and some had domestic violence charges. He was disappointed to find that none had any charges related to fire setting, though. He went on to current employees and added those with records to the list.

All in all, it appeared that Maui Sugar was not particular about its hiring practices—and, sitting in his air-conditioned office, he glanced out the window at the green of the nearby trees and reflected on the hot, dusty sugar mill and its sun-struck fields. No, they probably couldn't afford to be too picky.

He called Ferreira on his desk phone. "I've got a list of addresses going. How about you? Ready to take a drive out and knock on some doors?"

"Gimme another fifteen minutes," Ferreira said. "Do you want to follow up on the complaint letters, too, today?"

"No, let's do some drive-bys and see what we come across. We can go home from there, get to the complaint letters tomorrow."

"Sounds good, boss. Meet out in the lot in fifteen."

Stevens hung up, and his cell phone rang as if on cue, an unknown number. He didn't usually answer those, but maybe it was Lei, calling from that burner phone. He hadn't remembered to save the number as a contact.

"Hello?"

"Michael." The way Lei said his name, bitten off and spit out, let him know she wasn't happy. That was fine. He wasn't happy with her either. "Just got out of a meeting with Ohale and a couple of detectives from Vice. Apparently you called and told him I wasn't supposed to have anything to do with the Changs."

"I sure did," Stevens said, his temper flaring all over again. "What the hell are you doing over there?"

"I'm on a case. I told you. Nothing to do with the Changs, and I resent you policing me like this. Three days. Gambling and some sort of coercion. Omura authorized it."

"Why didn't you tell me yesterday, if you had nothing to hide?"

A long beat went by. "When would I have told you?" Lei's voice had dropped to a whisper. He couldn't tell what that whisper concealed. "At dinner with Dad and Jared? After, when we were making love? It's no big deal. I'll be home before you know it."

Behind Lei's anger he heard hurt, and in her whisper there was apology and a reminder of last night's incredible lovemaking.

Damn, he loved her, difficult as she was, and he just wanted her back—by his side, in his bed. Another lonely night without her didn't appeal. Stevens blew out a breath, relaxing. "I might have jumped to the wrong conclusion. You not telling me, the phone not working...it seemed like you might be going off on a personal mission."

She laughed, but it sounded strained. "I've got too much to lose. But I did want to tell you something. The baby kicked. Still kicking, in fact. I think we might have a hyper one on our hands."

"What? Isn't it too soon?" Stevens felt something welling up inside that he couldn't put a name to. It made him smile.

"No. Four months is when you can start feeling them move. And right in the middle of the meeting with the vice detectives, Baby started wiggling. I thought it was gas at first, but no." Stevens could hear a note of the same cocktail of wonder and excitement he felt in Lei's voice. "I ended up having to tell Ohale because he saw on my face that something had happened."

"I bet he was surprised."

"Not so much. He's happy for us—that's all." She paused. "We haven't talked about names."

"Depends on whether it's a girl or a boy."

"What depends? The name?"

"Yeah."

"Well, we should start thinking about it."

"Do you want to find out what the sex is?"

"I don't know. Do you?"

"I don't know."

"God." Lei laughed. "We're both too scared to know."

"I don't care, actually. As long as he or she is healthy—but you have to be okay, too." He hadn't expected the roughness that came into his voice.

"I'm fine. Healthy as a horse and twice as strong. Stop worrying."

"It'll be easier when you're back home." He cleared his throat. "Since you're over there, partying, I'm going to invite Jared over for drinking and poker."

"Partying? You should see the nasty dump I'm in. Nah, you have fun. I'll try to wrap this up as soon as possible. Then we can continue where we left off."

"Where we left off? You mean arguing?"

"No. In the bedroom." Her voice had gone husky. "I liked that thing you were doing...in the dark. I want to be the boss next time."

"Damn you, woman." He felt himself tightening in response to her voice, to the memory of the other night when he'd decided to get a little creative. Knowing they'd have the rest of their lives to explore every nuance of the pleasure their bodies could give each other still felt unreal to him. "I gotta go. Ferreira's waiting."

"And now you have a boner. My work here is done." She hung up with a laugh.

Stevens shook his head, smiling—but a little part of him wondered, as he slid the phone into his pocket, if he'd just been played.

THE DOORBELL of his apartment rang, an unfamiliar buzz, and the Fireman woke up, heart thundering. No one rang his doorbell.

He hurried to the door, alarmed. He applied an eye to the peephole and spotted the brown of a UPS uniform. He opened the door and signed for the package, carrying it inside after he'd relocked the dead bolt, thumb lock, and lever security bar behind him.

There was no return address, but the Fireman knew who it was from.

He got a knife and cut the tape on the package, peeling back the flaps. Inside, wrapped in bubble wrap, were several items and a printed-out letter.

To the Fireman: Here are the items you will need to breach the security of the house. This package is being delivered by one p.m. You have two hours to prep. You must be at the address at three p.m., when the man who stays in the house during the day leaves. You will have approximately ninety minutes from three p.m. to deactivate the alarm at the gate (code enclosed) neutralize the dog with the tranquilizer gun included, breach the house if needed (additional code enclosed), and set your fire. Best time to fire the house for optimal impact will be late at night. We will be watching the news tomorrow for results.

We have kept surveillance on the house for some time to

detect traffic patterns and have included some footage of the interior of the house so you can plan your ignition.

Place the enclosed cloth where it will be found after the fire.

We expect results, and we will reward them—we've included a bonus for being prompt. You can also expect consequences if you fail.

The Fireman felt his heart thumping an uneven tattoo as he set the written instructions and codes aside. This wasn't the same kind of excitement he got planning a cane burn. This was a family in their home. And he was going to try to kill them. For money.

The Fireman took out an object and unwrapped the bubble wrap. It was a sturdy black pistol with a box of tranquilizer darts taped to it. Another square packet turned out to be five thousand dollars in cash. Finally, there was a long length of loosely woven white linen cloth. He held it up, frowning, wondering what the significance was.

He took out another, smaller object. It was a thumb drive with a decal of flames decorating the side.

The blackmailer had a sense of humor.

The Fireman plugged the flash drive into his computer. In all his poverty, even in the worst months, he hadn't sold his computer. It was his only contact with the world. His entire social life was on the firebug forums, where he got to interact with other people obsessed with fire.

He clicked on the drop-down menu that opened and hit view files.

He clicked on exterior security first and got a bird's-eye view off the corner of the house of several vehicles coming and going: a silver Tacoma truck, an aging brown Bronco, and a huge black Ford F-150. That was the vehicle at the house most often, but as the instructions had said, a tall, silver-haired man came out of the house at three p.m., according to the time stamp on the video. He carried a baby in a car seat carrier out of the house, loaded it into the extended cab of the F-150, pulled out, and left for two hours, returning at five p.m.

At six p.m. a silver Tacoma arrived, and a slender, curly-haired woman got out, greeting the Rottweiler, which roamed randomly throughout the footage like a demonic djinn. At six-thirty p.m., the brown Bronco returned and a dark-haired man got out.

The Fireman grimaced as he saw the woman, carrying the baby, come down the stairs to kiss the man. They stood close together for a long moment, the man's arms around the woman and child. Even in the grainy pixilation of the feed, he could see the love between them.

"Jesus." He spat it like a curse, but found it had become a prayer. "Help me, God. I don't want to do this."

Was he really going to try to murder this family? It had been a hell of a lot easier to imagine how to do it when he'd thought only of the problem of the house and not who was inside. Dealing with just the challenge of setting a great fire, he'd been excited to do what he loved and get paid for it—until he was confronted with the human faces he was supposed to kill.

He switched to the interior surveillance and almost turned it off after a couple of minutes. There was no audio, but now, through the eyes of cameras in each room, he watched the woman and took in her quick laughter, her playful affection for the baby, and her husband. Even the grandfather and the dog began to look benign to him.

His mind scrabbled like a rat in a cage. There had to be some way out of this. His blackmailer seemed two steps ahead all the time, and clearly this family had been a target for a while.

Squelching the roil of mixed feelings, he watched the interior surveillance video again, this time ignoring the people and focusing on the layout of the rooms and the furniture. He got a paper and pen and sketched the layout. He watched the video again and drew the positions of the furniture.

The Fireman glanced up at the clock. He had only another hour to get ready, or he had no doubt the next ring on his doorbell would be the cops—or worse. Someone capable of planning this carefully was certainly capable of putting a bullet in his head.

Working fast, he updated his ignition plan and then packed the tranquilizer gun in the big black plastic bin with the rest of his supplies. He carried the bin out to his battered truck and lifted it into the back. He got into the truck and turned it on, finally making a decision.

He knew what he had to do.

LEI DROVE her rental car through the winding back streets of residential Hilo, heading for her old, familiar neighborhood with its narrow, weed-choked shoulders, buckling sidewalks, and sagging power lines. The run-down area was brightened by the colors of the old plantation houses—green, red, and mustard yellow trimmed in white with painted tin roofs and the arching lushness of *hapu`u* fern trees and sprays of blooming orchids decorating yards and driveways. Lei remembered every crack in those narrow sidewalks from all the running she used to do when she lived here.

Lei felt a tight band of anxiety and guilt around her chest as she thought of Stevens. She wished, oh, how she wished, that she had some other idea of how to find the shroud killer than pursuing Terence Chang. After her conversation with Ohale, she'd almost decided not to come this way. Her conversation with Stevens showed he was just as suspicious.

But she was here in Hilo. She had to at least take a look at Terence Chang. Just see what his routine was. Keep her options open. Let her gut tell her what to do. It rarely steered her wrong, and it was telling her to confront Terence Chang about the shrouds. How she would do that, she wasn't sure.

Lei had rented a car from Rent a Wreck Hilo, and the vehicle she'd chosen, a faded silver Toyota Corolla, felt like a cloak of invisibility. She'd stocked up for her surveillance with a big bottle of the

Vitaminwater she'd taken to drinking for the baby and a bag of beef jerky. Maybe not the healthiest option but the best she could come up with at the Minit Stop gas station, where, again, she'd paid cash and worn a green University of Hawaii ball cap, pulled low, to avoid surveillance cameras.

Lei knew exactly where she'd park. She'd chosen the spot when she'd been with the FBI on their last raid of the place and, in casing the big, old, plantation-style house for that police action, she'd checked for spots to do a stakeout if one was ever needed in the future.

She drove slowly but steadily past the house, doing an initial assessment.

Terence Chang had cleaned the old place up. The junked cars parked on the lawn were gone, and instead he'd erected a ten-foot-high chain-link fence. Lounging on the steps of the compound were two brindled pit bulls. Lei would never forget meeting the one that was Chang's personal pet. She'd almost had to shoot the beast.

The house had been freshly painted and repaired and was now a traditional dark green with white trim and sported a new roof. The lawn was neatly mowed and clear of any cover.

"Nice," Lei muttered. In spite of what the FBI and Hilo PD had been able to find out, Lei felt confident that Terence Chang was sending a message with the facelift to the property: There was a new crime boss in town, and he ran a tight operation.

Lei kept her speed steady as she passed, and then circled around and parked at the spot she'd chosen, behind a neighbor's hedge, where the car, pulled off the shoulder, would be out of view of the house.

By sliding down in her seat and leaning out the window, she could see past the hedge to the porch of the Chang house, where the pit bulls still snoozed.

Lei took in additional details: a locked, automated rolling gate; a closed, double-width garage, so there were probably a couple of cars parked there at least. She spotted a towering satellite antenna anchored to the roof.

He might be cleaning up the outside of the house, but it looked like he was ensuring he had the highest tech available, which meant anything could be happening inside. She couldn't see them, but he probably had exterior surveillance cameras.

She would if she were him.

Breaching the house wouldn't be easy, and what was visible was probably only a fraction of the defenses he had.

Lei opened the Toughbook laptop she'd brought over from Maui and punched up Chang's information. He had two cars registered: a black Tacoma truck and a baby blue Lexus.

Black Tacomas. They occurred way more than statistically likely in this corner of the world. Well, at least she knew which cars coming out of the garage to follow, because getting Chang from his vehicle was looking a hell of a lot easier than trying to get into his house.

CHAPTER SEVEN

STEVENS AND FERREIRA drove through Kahului in the Bronco. Ferreira played navigator, punching addresses into the GPS mounted on the dash.

"Seems like Maui Sugar's not paying much, if these addresses are anything to go by," Stevens said, mopping his brow with a forearm after their most recent stop, an employee fired for stealing some equipment. The maze of junked cars and illegally sublet semi-habitable shacks on the big lot in the middle of Kahului reminded Stevens of some of the neighborhoods he'd seen in third-world countries during his stint in the army.

"It's hard agricultural labor. Don't imagine it's any better anywhere else," Ferreira said. "I didn't like the situation with some of the kids there, though." They'd passed one of the dwellings, a room made out of an old Matson shipping container, and there had been at least six children under the age of five milling around with a few toys on a scrap of shag carpet inside. Windows cut in the metal sides provided the only ventilation, and a half-door held shut with an industrial-strength bolt kept the kids inside with a surly teen who eyed them through shaggy bangs, her ears plugged with headphones.

"I think I'll call Child Welfare to check the situation out. What did you think of Adeno Arias?"

They'd found the sometime-thief asleep on a futon under a mango tree in the backyard, covered by a beach towel. A nearby empty quart of Ocean Vodka lay next to him, telling its own tale. He'd been very hard to rouse.

"I don't think he has the wherewithal to plan these fires. Doesn't have a car. I don't think he's our man," Stevens said.

"Agreed." Ferreira jotted their impressions next to the man's name and address as Stevens followed the refined voice giving directions to their next stop, a three-story apartment building in Wailuku. A depressing beige when freshly painted, it now sported the ubiquitous rusty shade of blowing red Maui dirt.

"Kenny Rice," Ferreira read off the Department of Motor Vehicles information sheet. "Aged fifty-four. Not married. Fired for something they wrote up as 'negligence.'"

They parked the Bronco and marched up the metal exterior stairs to the man's door and knocked.

"What?" The door whipped open and a dark-complexioned man faced them, a beer belly barely contained by an undershirt straining over his belt line.

"Maui Police Department. We're looking for Kenny Rice," Ferreira said, holding up his cred wallet. Stevens just stood, hands on his hips, his holstered weapon and the badge clipped to his waistband more than enough ID for this civilian.

"Don't know him, but he lived here before," the man said.

"Got an ID for yourself?" Ferreira said. "We want to speak to him."

"Be right back." The door slammed.

"Nice guy," Ferreira said to Stevens. Stevens shrugged. He was feeling hot and annoyed. This kind of fishing expedition took so much time and seldom went anywhere. He wished he had some more staff to put to this kind of canvassing, but his station was just too small to spare anyone. Still, it was something to do, and it kept his mind off Lei...

The door reopened. The man dragged a frail-looking older woman in a flowered muumuu forward and handed over his driver's license. "I'm Frank Viela. This is my mother, Grace. Mama, tell them what you told me about Kenny."

"What you cops want with Kenny?" The woman's voice shivered with age and apprehension. "Kenny, he my cousin's boy. He's a good man."

"Just want to ask him a few questions about a case we're investigating, Aunty," Ferreira said, smiling with local-boy charm. "Anything you could tell us would help."

"Well, he lost this apartment when he got fired," Grace said, tweaking her elbow out of her son's hand. "He had to move."

"Do you happen to know where?"

"Over in Happy Valley, I heard," Grace said.

"Thanks so much for your help," Stevens said. "We appreciate it."

"He's on unemployment, so they will have his address," Grace contributed, batting rheumy eyes at Stevens.

"They're cops, Ma. They can figure it out," Frank said. He pulled her back from the door and shut it firmly behind them.

"Happy Valley," Stevens murmured as they clunked down the stairs. "Now, there's a misnamed spot."

"It didn't used to be so bad," Ferreira said, referring to the bottom of Iao Valley, where a low-income housing area had taken on a self-perpetuating cycle of drugs and urban decay.

"Well, Grace had one thing right. We should call the unemployment office and get his latest address."

Back at the Bronco, Stevens ran the engine and sorted through their notes as Ferreira called the state agency and procured the man's address. It wasn't far to the decrepit area. Stevens and Ferreira navigated down Main Street, the artery through old-town Wailuku, to the new address for Kenny Rice provided to them by the unemployment office. The road passed a series of coffee shops, pawnbrokers, and threadbare boutiques with hand-lettered signs and dipped down into a seedy neighborhood.

The area had a history of having been the first low-income housing on the island, and it was a haven for the unsavory, with broken culverts, graffiti-covered walls, and a series of barracks-like low-income apartments. The address the GPS guided them to was one of the regulation-height three-story buildings that populated the area. This one was painted pistachio green.

Stevens pulled the Bronco into a cracked asphalt lot, unembellished with even a palm tree. A row of listing steel mailboxes in front of their parking spot held the number they sought. "This is his place."

"Feeling like we're on a wild-goose chase," Ferreira said, unbuckling his seat belt.

"Yeah, guess it's been a while since either of us had to do so much old-fashioned shoe-leather police work," Stevens said with a grin. "Let's keep working through this list until five p.m. It's three now, so whatever we get done, we get done."

They got out, and Stevens scanned the empty lot. Happy Valley was a place where it never paid to get sloppy. He liked driving the old Bronco because the rust gathering on the back bumper and dents from a few chases just added to its island cruiser vibe, and the surf racks on top didn't scream "cop."

Stevens and Ferreira ascended a set of metal stairs on the outside of the building's chipped cement block exterior and knocked on the door of 3A, a thin plywood edifice marked with a spyhole in the middle.

No answer.

Stevens looked for a bell to ring, pushed it. He knocked again. They waited.

"Guess the guy's not home."

"We'll have to come back." Ferreira made a note on the clipboard he carried.

Stevens spotted the twitching of curtains in another unit as they moved back down the outside stairs. The hairs on the back of his neck rose the way they did when there was a gun on him.

"Let's wear Kevlar next time we come," Stevens said once they were inside the Bronco.

THE FIREMAN APPROACHED the home's address from downwind so as not to alert the dog. He'd come fifteen minutes early, so he could be sure the old man had taken the baby and left. From his treetop look-out, he used binoculars to watch the old man exit the house, baby carrier in hand. The man stowed the child in one of those click-on car seats, got into the truck, and fired it up. He must have hit a remote because the gate retracted, he backed the big vehicle up, turned around, and drove out.

The gate shut and the truck rattled down the driveway.

So far, so good.

The Fireman climbed back down the tree, a cumbersome busi-ness. He'd worn zip-up work coveralls with leather gloves and work boots, a cap pulled low. The outfit would camouflage his identity and provide protection from the hazards under the house, where he was planning to set the fire.

The blackmailer had told him there were no surveillance cameras except his own planted ones. The Fireman wasn't worried about being seen, though as usual, mud obscured his plates and he wore his billed cap low just in case. He pulled his vehicle into the driveway and punched in the gate code. He had no intention of facing the dog unprotected.

Sure enough, as the gate rolled open, the big Rottweiler trotted around the corner of the house, triangular ears pricked, its expression curious. It was not expecting a car to come in so soon after the old man's departure, the Fireman could tell. He pulled the truck forward toward the house and saw the dog's expression change.

It lowered its head, a ruff rising along its shoulders, and the barking that issued from its scarred barrel of a body echoed ominously inside his tin can of protection. It stalked toward his vehicle, barking. When the truck drew to a stop, the dog still came, stiff-legged, a growl like a grizzly bear vibrating its chest.

The Fireman rolled his window down partway, resting the tranquilizer pistol on the edge of the glass. He saw the amber gleam of intelligence in its eyes as the dog, still approaching, decided to jump. It gathered its huge body and leaped off the ground, aiming at his lowered window, and as it flew toward him, he pulled the trigger.

The dart buried itself all the way to the red-tufted hilt in the broad chest of the beast as it hit the side of the truck like a rhinoceros in full charge, snapping jaws reaching for him through the narrow gap of window. The truck rocked at the impact, and the Fireman recoiled, dropping the gun as the Rottweiler slid down the side of the vehicle to land on its feet, unharmed.

The Fireman rolled the window back up as the animal trotted away, turning to make another charge. The dog seemed to finally notice something was wrong. He saw it try to paw at the dart lodged in its chest, bending its head to try to grab the dart, but couldn't reach it.

His aim had been good. The red tuft protruded in the juncture of its neck and shoulder, sunk as deep as it would go.

The dog looked up at him again, and the Fireman felt his testicles shrivel at the look in its eyes. He could swear it was promising vengeance as it lay down carefully, resting its head on its paws, and still facing him, slowly closed its eyes.

He waited another five minutes.

He'd expected the Rottweiler to collapse in some way that he could be assured it was knocked out, but instead it had posed like an Egyptian sphinx, pointed right at him, its eyes shut like it was just having a tiny nap, waiting to sink its teeth into his leg as he tried to pass.

The Fireman opened his door carefully. No movement from the

dog. He extended a leg out onto the ground slowly, checking his watch. This had already taken fifteen minutes, longer than he'd budgeted. He lifted the pistol, took careful aim, and shot the dog again. He hit it right in the neck. It didn't move.

Two doses ought to hold the beast. If it died of a heart attack, so much the better. All he needed was to be undetected until he could torch the house.

He reached back into the truck and got out the bin of materials he'd brought for the fire, and still biting his tongue, the tranq gun lying on top of the bin, he walked up to the dog. He set the bin down, holding the gun on the dog.

He couldn't leave the darts in to be found. No movement, still, from the dog. He tweaked the darts out of its neck, hyperventilating.

No movement from the animal—it was out cold. He hurried on as quickly as possible.

He could always shoot it again, if he needed to, but ideally it would be waking up as the old man came back. Drugging it for too long would arouse suspicion.

The Fireman carried the bin to the opening in the latticework that covered the three feet or so of clearance below the house's post-and-pier construction. He pushed up his cap, flicked on the headlight he wore underneath, and crawled under the house. Carefully, he pushed the heavy bin ahead of him through the dirt.

It was dark in the crawlspace, with a faint musty odor like fresh mushrooms. Once in the center of the even rectangle of the house's footprint, the Fireman took out his hand-drawn map and oriented himself. Using it as a guide, he found the front entrance. Using the wide-bit drill, he bored up through to the subfloor, a three-inch-distance layer before the plywood of the floor. Pushing up with a battery-operated saw, he cut a rectangle in the subfloor and then, once more checking his map, he drilled all the way up through the floor above to create air-ventilation holes that would draw the flame up into the house.

Fire needed just a few things to blossom: an ignition source, fuel, and a lot of oxygen—and to get going hot and deadly, it needed a lot of everything.

Using the interior surveillance video, he'd been able to choose positions for the holes underneath a cabinet next to the front door. While not as good as having an ignition site directly in front of the door, it would have to do to block the main entrance.

He crawled on, boring four other sets of ignition and ventilation holes. Finally, he went back to the bin and got out the double-bagged Ziplocs of fuel.

The Fireman's back was hurting by then, his knees sore from the dirt and rocks, and his hands wouldn't stop the trembling they'd begun ever since the big Rottweiler hit the side of his truck. Still he pressed on, setting the bags of accelerant carefully up inside the subfloor. He was encouraged that he couldn't smell any fuel as he carefully inserted one bag per opening.

He'd fire the front door area first and give it the longest time to catch. Now that he'd done the prep work, all that remained was to set up the ignition of that first bag. Once the origin site was going, it would spread quickly to the others, especially with the nice updraft he'd created by drilling holes in the floor.

The Fireman had to crawl all the way back out from under the house to locate an electrical outlet. He kept the tranq gun at the ready and one eye on the dog as he searched, finally locating an outlet in the attached garage, hidden behind the washing machine. The washing machine seemed like a good place to leave the linen cloth he'd been told to plant at the fire—they'd trace the ignition source, and if he put it in the washer, they'd find it there, unburned.

He plugged the timer into the plug behind the washer and set it to one a.m., an hour when it was likely they'd be in bed. He plugged the extension cord into the timer and fed it through the wooden latticework back under the house.

Breaking a sweat in his hot coverall, he jogged back to the access point and checked his watch—he had only twenty minutes before the old man came back.

Under the house, he dragged the extension cord, with its peeled, exposed wires, through the dirt and fed it up into the subfloor. Using a staple gun, he attached the cord securely so it couldn't fall down and away from the bags of fuel.

Now he needed to set up his immediate ignition source. He made a pile of pure cotton balls and soaked them in a whole bottle of nail polish remover, pouring the remover out onto the balls.

This would smell, but he hoped the smell was familiar enough not to set off any alarms with the people inside.

He buried the exposed wires in the cotton balls and mounded them over the bag of fuel.

Then he crawled back out, assembled his tools and piled them into the bin, mentally ticking over the steps to ignition.

One a.m. would come, and the timer would click on, allowing electrical juice to flow down the cord and create a spark when the current jumped the gap on the exposed wires. The spark, which would be sustained, would ignite the fumes evaporating from the soaked cotton balls. The burning cotton balls would then melt through the plastic bag, causing the fuel to splash out and spread, flashing into flame with a delightful *whoosh*, licking up through the ventilation holes and spreading rapidly to melt the other fuel bags in a chain reaction.

The Fireman found himself smiling as he pushed the bin out from under the house and stood up. He couldn't wait to watch the whole thing.

His hands were occupied with the bin, the tranq gun lying on top of the lid. His eyes fell on the dog—it was looking at him.

Adrenaline flooded his body in a spurt that straightened his stiffened back and aching knees.

The dog blinked, and he saw it was still waking up. Its head wove back and forth and it tried to stand.

The Fireman ran for his truck with all the speed he could muster. He tossed the bin in the back, yanked the door open—and felt the dog hit him from behind as he lurched into the cab, screaming involuntarily. He was reduced to the gibbering terror he'd had as a child when a neighbor's pit bull had gotten him by the leg—he still carried the scars from that attack on his body, and on his psyche.

He felt the Rottweiler's jaws close on the back of the coverall and thanked God he'd worn the thick garment as he hauled himself inside the truck and yanked the door shut, slamming it hard on the dog's body.

It must have still been wobbly from the tranq because the Rottweiler let go and fell away, and he was able to get in and shut the door. He'd left the keys in the ignition and started it with a roar, looking out the window.

The dog was standing, but its head was down, its sides heaving, as he backed the truck up, suppressing an urge to run over the beast. Instead he drove past it and paused to punch in the gate code, keeping an eye on the dog in his rearview mirror.

It had collapsed onto its butt, still staring at him as if wishing it had the energy to give chase—but the gate opened and then closed behind his truck, and driving down the road, he felt triumph blow through his veins.

He would come back to watch. He wasn't going to miss this show for anything.

LEI WOKE WITH A LITTLE SNORT. She'd fallen asleep in the warm car, her chin resting on the edge of the window, where it needed to be to see Chang's front door. She blinked and lifted her phone to check the time—five o'clock.

It didn't appear she'd missed anything. The dogs hadn't even moved.

This stakeout had been a waste of time. The only information she'd been able to gather was that Chang's house was nearly impenetrable. She still had no idea of his patterns.

Lei yawned. Next to an oversensitivity to smells, needing a nap in the afternoon was her worst pregnancy symptom. That and having to pee, which she needed to do ASAP.

She turned on the rental car and headed back into downtown Hilo, making a call to the other detectives and letting them know she was going to be using the computer lab at South Hilo Station to try to track the online gambling.

CHAPTER EIGHT

STEVENS RUBBED Keiki's ears as the big dog sat beside him. She had been agitated all evening, whining and trotting around, and both he and Jared had tried to get her to settle. Kiet was down for the night long ago, and Stevens, Wayne, Pono, and Jared had been playing poker for some hours. He glanced at the clock above the sink —eleven p.m.

"Ante up," Wayne said. They each threw a five into the pot, and still studying his cards, Stevens rubbed the dog's head. He had two sevens and three mismatched number cards.

"Raise you three," Wayne said, swapping out two cards. The low overhead light gleamed on his silver hair and cast shadows beneath his craggy cheekbones.

"I'll match that," Jared said, leaning forward to toss his money into the round koa calabash they were using to hold the loot. When Stevens had set this up, he'd told them to each bring fifty in small bills, and the game was getting serious.

Pono took a sip of his beer, frowning. Stevens was pretty sure he did that when he thought he had a good hand. "Raise you five," Pono said.

Stevens narrowed his eyes at his Hawaiian friend. "Getting too rich for my blood. I fold." He set his cards down and leaned back, one hand on the dog's head, the other wrapped around a dwindling Longboard Lager.

"I call," Wayne said. Of the four of them, Wayne was the most unreadable, his rugged face blank.

Jared ended up taking the hand. Stevens lifted his beer in toast to the younger man. "Next round is on my bro," he said as Jared scooped the cash into a pile in front of him.

"Not a problem," Jared said. He got up and staggered a little as he made his way into the kitchen, coming back with another round of beers. "I think Lei should go out of town more often."

· "She'll be pissed to miss this, actually, and not be able to drink either. She loves a good game—right, Wayne?" Stevens had discovered the hard way that whatever Lei played, she played to win.

"She would hate to miss this," Wayne agreed. "But I'm glad she's on the Big Island right now so I can let it all hang out." He burped a huge belch, and they all laughed.

"She's staying away from the Changs, right?" Pono had a dent between his thick brows.

"Yep," Stevens said, squelching a pang of worry. "I made sure of it every way I can."

Wayne dealt the next hand, and his eyes, when they caught Stevens's, were serious. "Texeiras have long memories, and so do the Changs. I wish we could just all move on."

"The shrouds are what's worrying us." Stevens took a pull off his fresh beer. "We know there are more out there, and we don't know what he'll do next."

"Well, this place is about as secure as anywhere on this island," Pono said. "The only thing more I'd do is put in some surveillance cams."

Keiki nudged his thigh with her silky nose, and Stevens stroked her head again. "We used every penny we had moving in here and getting it minimally fixed up. The cameras are on the to-do list, but first we have to dig out from under some of our debt."

Pono waved away the beer Jared offered. "Nah. I gotta get on home. Got to work tomorrow. I better quit while I'm ahead." He brandished a fistful of dollar bills at them. "Next stop, Vegas."

Stevens looked over at Jared, who was counting his cash. "You shouldn't drive, bro. Spend the night on the couch."

"Don't mind if I do." Jared hadn't won much. He set down his handful of cash and stretched thick, corded arms high over his head. He yawned, his jaw cracking. "Had another fire today. Thought Maui was going to be mellow, but there's always something cookin' in Kahului."

Pono stood up. "Still. Must be better than LA." He shoved his take into a back pocket.

"You got that right. Mike and I both are glad to have escaped the Madland, as you locals call it."

They said their goodbyes, Wayne and Pono departing at the same time. Stevens went to the linen closet and found a sheet and a blanket and came back. Jared was already down on the couch, his eyes shut, and he didn't move when Stevens approached. Too much beer and hard work had taken a toll.

Stevens shook out the blanket, a thin cotton coverlet, and draped it over Jared. Doing so reminded him of all the days when, as kids, he'd looked in on his brother after their dad died.

Jared had taken their father's death hard. Harder even than Stevens had. Stevens remembered the sight of his little brother, four-teen then, sleeping in bed with their dad's battered yellow fire hat. He'd covered him up then, too, without a word.

No wonder Jared had gone on to be a firefighter. But Stevens had needed more complex bad guys to fight than that hot, blind, gobbling enemy.

Stevens went on through the house, checking the locks. Keiki whined near the front door, sniffing at the floor.

"C'mon, girl. Let's go to bed." He summoned her with a snap of his fingers and made one final stop, to check on Kiet.

The nightlight lit the baby's room with a soft yellow glow. Stevens tiptoed over to the crib.

Kiet was asleep on his back, dark hair like feathers around his head, arms flung wide in utter relaxation. The baby's soft pink mouth worked an imaginary nipple in his sleep, the white blanket Stevens had covered him with still in place.

Stevens felt a constriction around his chest, a tightness in his throat. His son was so beautiful. He couldn't resist reaching in to touch the baby's hair, the feeling like the finest silk under his finger-tips. As it always did, that hair reminded him of Anchara and brought the complicated maelstrom of feelings thinking of her murder always brought—guilt, sorrow, anger, regret.

He swallowed the lump in his throat and tiptoed out, shutting the door.

Jared had begun to snore in the living room, a soft rumble.

Stevens smiled at that, and went into the bedroom. Keiki pressed close, right behind him, and he closed the door and turned on the baby monitor on his side of the bed.

"Relax, old girl." He pointed to Keiki's spot on their bed with her special blanket. She hopped up, but she was still looking at him, her eyes worried, when he turned off the light. He patted her flank and she finally lay down. "Maybe I'll take you to the vet tomorrow. You've been acting weird all evening."

CHAPTER NINE

KEIKI'S BARKING BROUGHT Stevens abruptly upright. The smell of smoke, with its terrifying memories of another fire he'd lived through, pumped adrenaline through his body as he bolted out of bed.

The floor felt roasting hot on his bare feet as Stevens yanked the bedroom door open, still half awake but driven by terror for Jared and Kiet.

A wall of smoke swirled in, searing his eyes and blinding him. He dropped to his knees, coughing convulsively.

"Mike, get on the floor!" Jared's voice. He was too blinded to see, but his brother's voice came clearly to him. "I've got the baby!"

"Oh, thank God," Stevens tried to say, but nothing came out but a croak as his throat seemed to shut down. He lay flat on his belly, and through slit, streaming eyes, saw the shadow of his brother crawling toward him.

"Get Keiki and let's go out through the kitchen," Jared said, crawling by rapidly. "I don't see any fire by that door." Stevens wiped his eyes on his shirt and could see the lump that was Kiet stowed against Jared's chest inside his T-shirt, held tight with one arm. "I'm taking the baby out!" Jared's voice cut through the roar.

"Follow me. Stay low. Find something to put over your face." He disappeared, obscured by a back draft of black smoke.

Flames shot up inside Stevens's bedroom with a roar, igniting underneath the small table in front of the window and blocking it as an escape.

"Kitchen door," Stevens muttered, trying to orient. Jared had already disappeared. He looked around for Keiki and was dismayed to see she'd crawled under the bed. The bed was pretty close to going up in flames.

Stevens crawled back. He hauled the dog out by her collar using brute force and ripped a pillowcase, already hot, off the bed and covered the big dog's head, hoping that she'd do better by not being able to see. He pulled his arms out of his T-shirt, pushing it up over his nose and mouth. Keiki crouched down, whimpering with terror, and tried to pull away. One hand on the hot floor, the other on the dog's collar, towing her, Stevens crawled toward the kitchen.

The living room was well on its way to gone. He couldn't see anything but flames in that direction.

He tried to decide where to turn outside his bedroom. Was the kitchen to the right, or was it left? He couldn't remember, and he couldn't open his weeping eyes, and he couldn't breathe. Keiki felt like two hundred pounds of deadweight at the end of his arm.

Someone grabbed him by the shoulder. "It's Jared. Come on, Mike. Grab my shirt." Jared's voice was muffled by something over his face. Stevens blinked, trying to see what was going on, where they were going.

"It's okay to shut your eyes. Lie on your belly and crawl with me. Just stay right next to me," Jared yelled hoarsely. "And let go of that dog if you have to. Come on!"

Leave Keiki? No way.

Stevens dug deep for more strength. His brother had already gotten Kiet out and had come back for them. It was going to be okay if he could just get himself and Keiki outside. He pressed close enough to touch his brother and crawled after him, giving an awkward heave every foot or two, hauling the dog's weight until finally he felt fresh air, a touch like a balm on his face, breath like diving into cool water filling scorched lungs as he rolled out the kitchen door, hauling Keiki after him.

Somewhere off in the distance, a timpani against the roar of hungry fire, he could hear sirens.

"Come out a little farther from the house." Jared's voice. "It's going up fast. I left my turnouts in the car. I'm going to try to knock some of the fire down."

Turnouts. Knock the fire down. Meaningless gibberish in the scope of what was happening.

Stevens crawled forward a few more feet and collapsed on his face on the cool grass. He gasped at the fresh air and convulsed with more coughing.

"Kiet?" he managed to get out.

"Wayne has him. He's okay."

Stevens lifted his head enough to see Wayne, cradling and patting the baby against his shoulder, way back against the fence. The baby was crying, great, big, healthy-sounding yells. That was a very good thing.

Stevens lowered his face into the grass and felt tears filling his scorched eyes. Their home. Burned. Everything they'd been trying to build destroyed again.

This was no accident, and they'd barely made it out alive. He was pretty sure there was a shroud lying around somewhere.

Lei. He had to call her, but his phone was gone, just one of the many things he'd think of needing and find had been burned. He remembered that constant disoriented feeling all too well. He crawled toward Wayne. "Phone?" he croaked, reaching out his hand.

LEI WOKE to the chattering of mynah birds in the huge banyan outside the motel. Somewhere not far away, she heard the shrill chirp of the invasive coqui frogs that had emigrated from Puerto Rico to the Big Island and made it their home. Warm, leaf-dappled sunlight fell through the louvered window whose drapes she'd forgotten to pull last night.

She'd gone to bed late after putting in hours at the South Hilo Station computer lab, searching through scores of cases on the secure computers. The good news was she'd been able to find some patterns and put together a list of victims and complainants to interview today. Not only that, she'd identified the two knee-breakers as small-time criminals from the Hilo area. She had names and addresses to call on.

She was actually working the case, and getting somewhere, too.

Lei rubbed her eyes, then shut them again. There was nothing too urgent going on today. She planned to set up a distance-feed surveillance cam on Chang's house so she didn't have to waste hours in the car in the hot sun. Then she'd see if she could get one of the other detectives to go out on some interviews with her.

She felt that funny feeling in her stomach, the twitching like gas bubbles.

The baby was awake, too.

She slid her hand under her sleep tee onto the smooth skin of her waist, pressed down on the hard, round bulge of her uterus.

There it was. A fluttering like a moth against the palm of her hand. She held that movement in her hand for a long moment, gently feeling around. She pulled up her shirt. If she lifted her head and sighted down her body, she could see where the baby was growing, a slight rise between her hipbones making a round shape as firm as a grapefruit and about as big.

Curious whether she could see the baby kicking, she pulled off her sleep tee and propped herself up on her elbows, watching the expanse of pale ivory skin that ended at her panties.

There it was again, that silvery movement. This time Lei could even see it happening, a staccato beating that jiggled the skin of her belly. "You must be hungry or something, Baby," she said aloud, and swung her legs to the side of the bed. "Can't believe I'm talking to you, but it's obvious you're really in there, doing your thing."

She smiled as she stood, feeling happy as she imagined Kiet and his brother or sister together. She couldn't wait to show her belly moving to Stevens. The message light was pulsing on her phone, but she needed a shower before she dealt with anything more to do with work.

She took a long shower and washed her hair. She'd noticed it was growing in fuller and even curlier, something the pregnancy books said to expect. Like she needed more hair. Her stomach fluttered again. "Okay, finding food, Baby," Lei said aloud.

She dressed and scooped up the phone, unplugging it from the charger, and loaded it into her purse along with her weapon and creds.

She didn't listen to the message until she had eaten a full breakfast of bacon and eggs and was sipping her second cup of decaf coffee.

Stevens's voice was so hoarse it was almost unrecognizable.

"He burned down the house." *Cough, cough.* "We got out, but he burned down the house. Call me!"

Lei's belly tightened so hard she almost hurled the breakfast back up all over the table. She took deep, slow breaths so as not to do that and looked at the time of the message: 1:35 a.m. She had the ringer off and had slept right through the crisis.

Twin demons of terror and guilt stabbed her.

Lei called his phone number back, but it went to voice mail. Then she checked the number the message had come from and realized it was her father's phone. She called it back, trying not to hyperventilate, wrapping her hand tightly around the poky tines of a fork to keep herself in her body.

"Dad, it's Lei. Oh my God, I just got Michael's message! Is he okay?"

"Aw, Sweets, your house is gone."

"Is Michael okay? The baby? Keiki?" Her voice had gone high

and tinny, and her sweating hands could hardly hold the phone as her vision telescoped down to a dot.

"Everyone's okay." He used a gentle tone. "They made it out okay."

"Oh, thank God!" She focused on trying to breathe.

"Jared was spending the night, and good thing he was. He got them all out okay. It was a bad fire, honey, and the whole place went up unbelievably fast."

"Was anyone hurt?"

"Keiki and Stevens went to the hospital for burns and smoke inhalation, but they're both recovering. They're going to be a little bald for a while, but okay. In fact, Mike's right here and wants to speak to you."

Lei squeezed the fork, feeling her terror recede, leaving her shaky and queasy in its wake. The big breakfast had been a mistake.

"Lei." The croak of his voice brought tears springing to her eyes. She stood up in agitation, ripping a twenty out of her wallet and throwing it on the table.

"Oh my God, Michael. I'm so sorry I had the phone off! I just got your message." She walked rapidly out of the restaurant to stand on the sidewalk in the shade of the banyans. She paced back and forth to work off the adrenaline. The baby kicked, and she realized it was feeling everything she was.

"I'm okay. We're all alive and we're gonna be fine. But the house, Lei." His voice cracked and broke. "Everything we had. Gone."

Lei shut her eyes, breathed in through her nose, out through her mouth. She reached up to clasp the rough, white gold medallion around her neck as she walked back toward her car, feeling her heart rate come down as she deliberately controlled her responses. "It's just stuff. It came easy; it went easy. We have each other."

"I know. I can hardly talk." He coughed, and it hurt her to hear the sound like ripping cloth. "I'm on oxygen, if I need it, for a couple days. Kiet is totally fine. Jared got him out first. We're here in Wayne's cottage and we're okay, but Keiki and I got pretty singed."

"This has to stop," Lei said. She got into the car and stared out the window, feeling blind and deaf to anything but this one thought. "This has to stop."

"I love you. Come home," Stevens croaked.

"I love you, too. I'll come. Just as soon as I can," she said. "I will be there as soon as I can." She closed the phone and whipped the car around, out into traffic.

CHAPTER TEN

THE FIREMAN OPENED the bin from yesterday's fire. He sorted the few tools remaining back into the tool chest: the staple gun, the tranquilizer pistol, the empty bottle of nail polish remover, the plastic bag the cotton balls had been in.

He could have left everything, including the bin, and it would have been obliterated by that masterpiece of a fire he'd set. Sure, they would find out it was arson, but that didn't matter. In fact, the blackmailer had wanted him to leave a message at the scene. That fire had done exactly what he wanted it to, right down to leaving the family a way out.

He sat back on his heels, replaying in his mind the scene he'd watched last night.

From his perch in the tree, he'd known they were out when the old man had run around to the backside of the house where the kitchen door was out of his view. He'd reappeared holding the baby —someone had carried it out to him. A few minutes later two men and the dog had appeared, one on his feet, the other crawling.

Where was the woman? He remembered the twitch of panic he'd felt as he swung the glasses around the scene of the blaze—and realized her truck wasn't there. Hadn't been the whole time.

She wasn't at the house. So much the better. He'd released a breath of relief. He didn't want that on his conscience. Nor anyone's death, in fact. He'd already had nightmares about the homeless man, gobbled by the Bitch. So he'd left a way out, and burned the house so dramatically that he was pretty sure the blackmailer would be satisfied. It was the best he could do for them.

He would know soon if it was enough.

STEVENS LAY BACK on the couch in Wayne's little cottage, sucking oxygen through a cannula into his sore lungs, and trying to recover from talking to Lei. His throat was still so painful, the tissues inflamed.

"She said she's coming home as soon as she can," Stevens said to Wayne, who was sitting with the baby on his lap and trying to feed him rice cereal. The spackle-like mixture was ending up on Wayne's shirt and all over the baby's hands and face as Kiet kept trying to grab the spoon.

"Of course she is," Wayne said. "Little man, we're making a mess here," he said to Kiet. "I really miss that bouncy seat. Soon as I'm done and cleaned up from this, I gotta go to the store and buy him a new one and more formula and diapers. Good thing I had some extra stuff out here."

"Thanks, Wayne. Don't know what we'd do without you." Stevens inhaled through his nose, which hurt less. He was needing less of the oxygen, but every time he exerted himself, he realized his body just wasn't getting all it needed right now.

He shuddered, remembering the experience of last night. That first big waft of smoke, when he'd opened the bedroom door, had seared his throat and lungs, causing them to constrict. By the time the EMTs got to him, he was almost unconscious, but not so far gone that he didn't remember the struggle to breathe as they strapped a mask over his face and turned on oxygen. Pain medication had helped him relax enough to get more of the oxygen into his system.

He needed to take it easy for just a day or two and let his burns recover. He looked down at his bandaged chest, hands, and knees.

He checked on Keiki. She was sleeping, still under some anesthetic from her burn treatment. She'd been intubated, and the mobile vet had treated her here. The side he'd dragged her on had lost most of its hair.

Thank God for Jared. He was pretty sure none of them would have made it out without his brother's cool head and quick action.

"All done." Wayne carried the baby to the little sink, wetted a paper towel, and wiped him down. "Hold him, will you? I gotta change my shirt."

"Hey, buddy." Stevens took Kiet, who grinned and reached for Stevens's blistered face as he sat up carefully. One side of Stevens's hair was mostly burned off, but Kiet's expression of delighted curiosity was as happy as usual. He folded the child close in spite of wriggling protests. "Thank God you're safe," Stevens muttered into the baby's tender neck.

Wayne cleared his throat, having reappeared in a clean T-shirt. "Okay, I'm going out to get the baby stuff. Got anything you need?"

Stevens gave a bark of a laugh. "Well, if you hadn't loaned me some clothes, I'd be naked right now. So yeah, maybe pick up a few things to wear. Mainly I need a new phone. Grab me a minutes-only burner and keep all the receipts. I'll get on the phone with the insurance company, see what's going to be covered."

"Sounds good." Stevens's father-in-law left, and as he did, Stevens glimpsed movement outside. He stood up with the baby, gasping involuntarily as his scorched feet hit the floor. Wayne had loaned him socks to go over the bandages, but the skin was tender. He walked to the little front porch and sat on the top step with the baby on his lap, looking over at the black hole where their house had been.

It was easier to think of the foul-smelling mounds of charred rubble as a black hole than to remember what it used to be. The fire crews were long gone, but the unpleasant smell of wet, burned wreckage lingered.

"We didn't have long to get too attached to it, did we?" Stevens asked the baby. "It's just stuff, like your mama said." Kiet flexed his legs, sticking out his tongue. His simple vitality was soothing to Stevens's ravaged emotions.

Stevens's eyes still stung and his vision was blurry at times, but he could see Tim Owen and Jared in their yellow turnouts, sifting through the remains.

Jared spotted him and raised a hand. In the chaos of last night, they hadn't spoken since their dramatic escape from the house. Jared crunched through the rubble and approached them.

"Hey, bro!" He took off his heavy hat, setting it on the step below Stevens. "How ya doing?"

Stevens felt his smile painfully in the tightness of his facial skin. "Glad to be alive."

"Little guy's looking no worse for wear," Jared said, as Kiet, gurgling, reached for his uncle.

"Thanks to you," Stevens said. "Not sure I could have got us out without you."

Jared's blue eyes crinkled and he shrugged, self-deprecating. "I should have been onto the fire sooner. I was sleeping so hard from all that beer. I didn't wake up until things were well on their way in the living room. I saw your door was closed and knew you'd have a few minutes, and Kiet was closer to the fire, so I went there first. Glad I did."

"Me too."

"So Tim thinks the fire was arson."

Stevens snorted. "'Course it was."

"And you're not gonna like this. He found one of those shrouds in the washing machine."

"Not surprised." Hot rage boiled down Stevens's veins, and he tightened his arms protectively around the baby. "This has to stop."

He thought of Lei's voice as she said that and wondered if that was what she'd been feeling, too.

"Tim's figuring out what the point of origin was. He thinks, from what I told him, it was by the front door in the living room. He's done a depth test on the wood left to confirm, and the char is deepest there."

"Tell him to coordinate with Pono. Pono's been in charge of the shroud investigation."

"I already did. Meetings, talks, and such are underway." Jared sat on the bottom step. "I shouldn't be too close to the baby," he said, leaning away when Kiet reached a hand for his hair. "We pick up all kinds of chemicals walking around in fires. That's why I never bring my turnouts into the house."

Stevens wasn't done talking about the night before. "You knew just what to do. I panicked when I realized the house was on fire, yanked the door open, and once I got that big draft of smoke, I was pretty much out of it. If I'd been thinking straight...Dad always told us to stay low, be careful opening doors if there was a fire."

"You get a pass. You'd already been through that other fire. That'll mess with a man's head. Besides, you've been looking for a way to give me a chance to save your life for years. Since we were kids, in fact." Jared grinned.

"Ha-ha, right." Stevens made a gesture as if to punch his brother, brought up short by the reminder of chemicals and his bandaged hands.

The lifted purple truck Pono drove pulled up the driveway, and they watched as Lei's burly ex-partner approached.

"The morning after a good poker game is always a little rough," Pono said as he reached the porch.

Stevens laughed a hoarse rasp. "Yeah, that was some game last night."

"So I'm up to speed with Tim Owen on what he's found so far," Pono said. They all looked at the young man dragging a metal sledge through the rubble to load with items as he continued sifting for evidence. "What's interesting is that he's sampled the accelerant. Preliminary reading shows it's the exact same mixture that was used on the cane fires."

Kiet chose that moment to get restless, fussing and writhing. "Why don't we go inside and you can get my statement," Stevens said. "I'll give this guy a diaper change."

"Never thought I'd hear that in a sentence." Pono chuckled.

"I'm back to work." Jared loped off as Pono came up the steps. Pono pulled open the screen door for Stevens, loaded with the baby and awkward with his bandaged hands.

"Can you do the diaper? Want me to help?"

"Nah, got it covered." Back in the cottage, Stevens put the baby on a towel on the couch and changed him while telling Pono the series of events. "Come to think of it, Keiki was acting funny all evening—running around, wouldn't settle down. She must have smelled something. Wish I'd paid more attention."

Pono flipped his notebook shut. "I know. I was there. How'd the arsonist get past her?"

"Don't know. But Keiki wasn't herself—that's for sure." The big Rottie raised her head at the sound of her name. "Yeah, girl, wish you could talk."

Keiki lowered her head with a deep, sad-sounding sigh. Pono frowned. "She looks pretty beat-up."

"She's got a few more battle scars, that's for sure, and the vet said she's getting up there for a Rottweiler. I dread how Lei's going to take it when she passes."

"Speaking of your wife—where the hell is she? I thought she'd be back by now."

"She didn't get my message until this morning. She said she'd come as soon as she could." As Stevens said that, he felt the same prickle of alarm, remembering her voice when she said, *"This has to stop."*

"Well, I hope she hasn't gone all *lolo* and taken on the Changs by herself," Pono said with a forced chuckle.

Stevens glared up at him. "Leaving me here to take care of the baby?" Neither of them, looking at each other, could make a joke of it. "I better call her. I'll tell her about the arson, the mixture of accelerant."

"Let me hold my *hanai* nephew, then," Pono said, and scooped Kiet up with the ease of a practiced dad.

Stevens borrowed Pono's phone and dialed the memorized number of the burner Lei had given him. She didn't pick up, and he felt agitation spiking his heart rate. He told himself she was probably at the airport and couldn't get reception.

"Lei, I'm on Pono's phone and just wondering what your ETA is. Kiet and I are hanging out at your dad's cottage, and there's a lot going on with the investigation. Pono says the accelerant used on the house is the same mixture as the cane fire burns, so maybe it's the same arsonist. Anyway, call me and let me know when to expect you." He hung up and took the baby from Pono without meeting his eyes. "I'm sure she's on her way back."

Pono shook his head. "*Chee,* brah. Sure hope so."

LEI FOUND herself in front of the Chang compound without any real idea how she got there.

She pulled up in her spot next to the hedge and got an eye on the property. Early morning. The dogs were sitting on the porch, alert. Still no signs of movement inside. One of the dogs spotted the hood of the car and trotted down the steps to investigate, a porch she well remembered storming up with the FBI team just a couple of years ago.

Lei shut her eyes and leaned her head on the steering wheel, considering her options.

She could continue with her current plan, which was to surveil the house, figure out Chang's traffic patterns, and find a way to grab him when he was on the move.

She could try to get help from her FBI friends or friends at the station, come up with some reason to search Chang's house, and let him know she was onto him.

Or she could do what she'd done with Healani Chang when the vendetta against her family was first revealed, walk up to the door and have a talk.

She made up her mind.

Lei reached into the backseat for her duffel bag. She strapped on an ankle holster with a small, unregistered snub-nosed six-shot already loaded in it. She clipped a knife in a sheath onto her belt and strapped into a Kevlar vest. She'd bought a larger one, so it came all the way down to her hipbones, making sitting in it awkward, but she had someone else to worry about now, and coverage was key. Short of getting shot in the head, she ought to be able to survive this confrontation.

"Because this has to stop," Lei said aloud. "Baby, it just has to stop."

Baby had nothing to add.

Lei strapped her shoulder-holstered weapon onto the outside of the vest and clipped her badge onto the front in plain view. And, finally, she scraped her unruly curls into a ball and anchored her hair with a rubber band. She was ready.

Lei got out of the car, slid the keys into her pocket, and walked casually to the front of the gate.

The dogs went apeshit, leaping off the porch and flying down the driveway to fling themselves at the wire, baying and howling an alarm.

Lei set her hands on her hips, legs spread, and waited.

The front door opened, and Terence Chang came out onto the porch. He looked impossibly young in a pair of gray sweats and a white T-shirt, his black hair spiky with sleep, and Lei remembered he couldn't be more than twenty-five. He clapped his hands, and the dogs shut up and trotted back to stand beside him on the porch.

"Lei Texeira," he said. "Kinda early for a raid, isn't it?"

"I just want to talk to you." She pitched her voice normally, and the dogs barked at the sound of it. He clapped his hands again, and they slunk away to lie down on beds on the end of the lanai.

"You what?" He walked down the steps toward the gate, and Lei imagined pulling her weapon and pegging him two in the chest, one in the head, like a Mafia executioner. The fantasy was so vivid that she blinked when he was still standing, and right in front of her. "What do you want?"

"I need to talk to you. A police matter."

He looked around. "You cops travel in packs. Where are the rest of them?"

"Just me this time." Lei kept her voice flat and uninflected. "We have some unfinished business."

"Yes, we do." He matched her tone. "Okay, come in."

"I'd rather you came with me. We can go somewhere private."

He snorted, and she realized his brown eyes were as hard as his grandmother Healani's had been. "I'll bet you'd like that. But no. You want to talk to me; you can come inside and sit down. We'll act all civilized, because that's how I roll." He'd been carrying a bunch of keys, and he unlocked a small gate next to the big retractable one.

Lei walked in, and the dogs surged up off their beds and swarmed down the stairs, barking. They surrounded her. "I say the word and they'll rip your throat out," Chang said.

"I expect no less." Lei kept her eyes unwavering on his. "Lead on."

He snapped his fingers, and the dogs retreated to either side of him as he led the way back up onto the porch. He held the grilled steel front door open. "After you."

Lei went ahead of him, stifling the fearful knowledge that she could be walking to her own execution. She was gambling with a pair of twos, but the right bluff could win her the game. A prickling at the back of her neck reminded her that he was right behind her and so were the dogs.

The interior was not as dim as she remembered. The place had been redecorated: white walls, a deep burgundy Persian rug, couches in pebbled chocolate leather, a wall-mounted flat screen.

After so long and so much death, here she was, in the living room of the enemy.

"Have a seat." He gestured to a couch.

Lei still stood, assessing. "Where is everybody?"

Every other time she'd been at this house, it had been a teeming beehive of activity and relatives, all armed and dangerous.

Terence Chang took a seat in what was plainly his usual spot, a designer leather chair facing the TV. "I live by myself now." One of the dogs, the brindled one that Lei recognized from the raid a few years ago, sat beside Chang and leaned on his leg.

Lei's eyes had adjusted to the interior light, so she chose a spot on one of the couches nearest the door. She was still feeling her way, considering what to do. There wasn't a blueprint for any of this. "You've made quite a lot of changes around here."

"Tutu left me the place and the business. I'm running it my way now."

She gazed at him. Chang had a handsome face, mixed heritage evident in the olive tan of his skin, flat cheekbones, and full lips. His tilted eyes were guarded but intelligent. She thought back to his belligerence and angry threats against her when he'd been in captivity with the FBI.

"We have a history, you and I."

"Inherited. I've got no beef with you."

"That's the first time I've heard that."

"Well, after that other situation, I took stock of my life. I was on probation for two years, as you know, and I cleaned house. Literally. Decided what I was going to do different, and one of the main things was to go straight. I have no need of the family business."

Lei sat back. "I don't believe you."

"Believe what you want. If you had anything on me, you'd be here guns blazing, looking for an excuse to blow my head off." He leaned forward, hands between his knees, eyes intent. "Why *are* you here?"

"Someone's trying to kill me and my family, and I think it's you." Now Lei leaned toward him as well. She narrowed her eyes, her hand landing on her weapon. "I can kill you right now and walk away with no one the wiser."

"I live alone, but I have surveillance cameras and an alarm company. You don't get to be who I am without backup. This whole thing is being recorded, and I've got an alarm button right here." He held up what looked like a TV remote. "It dumps the surveillance footage off-site to a safe location, so don't think you can go erase it."

Lei sat back again, smiled humorlessly. "You were always the smartest of the bunch."

"So they tell me."

A long pause as Lei tried to read him. She couldn't see anything but a young man, extraordinarily self-contained, his hand stroking the head of his dog. She saw tenderness in that hand, intelligence in those eyes. Maybe he had changed from the hate-filled kid she remembered.

"Then maybe you know who's stalking me and my family and leaving shrouds as a calling card."

"Maybe I do."

Lei's head jerked in surprise. "Go on."

"What do I get out of this?"

Lei felt a smile pull up one side of her mouth. "Maybe you don't know it, but you've been under both Hilo PD and the FBI's microscope for some time now. I can guarantee that all-seeing eye will be moving on to other targets if you aren't our guy."

"Of course I know I'm being monitored. I can't fart without getting pulled over in Hilo. And you've got some pretty good hackers, too, always trying to drill into my businesses. But they're all clean. Because I'm clean." He held out open hands. "Nothing on me. No blood, drugs, whores, gambling. That's the other branch of the Chang family."

"What other branch?" Lei frowned.

"Who else do you know that's a Chang with a long memory? Someone who has good reason to hate you?"

Lei frowned. She thought of the young man with striking hazel eyes who'd tried to date her long ago, and his sister who'd gathered information by getting a job at her aunty's restaurant in California. "Ray Solomon. Anela Chang. Haven't thought of them in years."

"Well, they've thought of you," Terence said.

"Holy shit," Lei breathed. "Why are you telling me this?"

"You know the old saying, the enemy of my enemy is my friend?" He sat back and steepled his fingers. "I've gone straight. But the Chang family enterprises are alive and well, under new management."

"I thought Ray was in a wheelchair." Lei winced internally, remembering she'd put him there.

"Yes, and it hasn't sweetened his outlook, nor impaired anything but his legs."

"And Anela?"

"She was always the real brains of those two."

"So when did this begin?"

"I think Ray began his power grab while he was doing time for his attack on you. For a while, I was having trouble figuring out what I was going to do. I was angry, lost without Tutu's leadership. I thought I'd keep things going in the family business—but as soon as I got out from under the FBI's microscope, I discovered everything was already under his and Anela's thumbs. I'd been squeezed out."

"So much for growing a conscience and going straight."

"I never said I grew a conscience." He shrugged, a hard light in his eyes telling Lei he was, first and foremost, a Chang.

"Now all I need is a location where I can find Ray and Anela." Lei fixed him with an unblinking Texeira stare.

CHAPTER ELEVEN

THE FIREMAN HAD FALLEN into a light doze in front of the TV, watching the news, when the shrill buzz of the doorbell woke him.

His heart went into overdrive, and he clutched his chest, willing that overactive organ to calm as he hoisted himself out of the rump-sprung couch. At the door, he applied his eye to the keyhole and, once again, saw the brown of a UPS uniform.

He signed for the package and relocked the door behind the man. His heart rate hadn't gone down, and his hands were sweaty as he carried the package over to the table and used a kitchen knife to slit the tape.

Unfolding the flaps of the box, he uncovered rubber-banded stacks of cash and another folded note.

Hello, Fireman. Nice fire, but they got out alive. You aren't off the hook from this until you get the job done. This time I want a copy of your fire plan. The good news is, they haven't left the property, and they're all in that tiny cottage. It shouldn't be too hard. The UPS man will be back to pick up from you tomorrow morning. Enclose the plan in the included delivery

envelope and I'll let you know if it's approved. Will provide
you more tech support as needed.

A flat-rate delivery envelope was at the bottom of the box. The Fireman took out the bundled cash. Counted it. He now had eighteen thousand dollars in his pillowcase, more than he'd ever had in his life—but he was supposed to keep going after this family.

His hands were clammy and trembling as he counted the cash again. He had until tomorrow to figure out another ignition plan, and right now, he couldn't imagine approaching that property again, crawling with investigators who were looking for him.

Wendy Watanabe, his favorite news reporter, was chirpily reviewing the results of the local election. She then switched seamlessly to another topic. "Tragedy almost struck on Maui late last night when the home of two of Maui's finest police officers was burned to the ground. Sergeant Lei Texeira was away from the residence on an assignment, but her husband, Lieutenant Michael Stevens, their infant son, and their dog barely escaped an extremely aggressive blaze triggered by arson. If not for the quick action of Lieutenant Stevens's brother, Jared, a firefighter who happened to be spending the night, the story would be even more tragic for this couple who have already lived through one blaze on Maui. Lieutenant Stevens is still injured from the fire and refused comment, but I was able to get Jared Stevens to talk about the fire. Jared, thank you for answering a few questions."

The camera swung to a young man's face, chiseled and handsome. He was wearing yellow fire gear and he took off his hat, tucking it under his arm and running a hand through dark brown hair. Bold blue eyes looked into the camera as Jared said, "I was just doing what I do. Frankly, I feel bad I didn't wake up sooner and couldn't do more to get the fire under control."

"Tell us how it got started."

"Well, we're still investigating, so you might want to ask Maui

County Fire Investigator Tim Owen for a few words. I was sleeping in the living room and woke up to the blaze." Jared described how he'd carried the baby out first and then helped his brother. "By the time the rest of the fire-suppression team got there, the house was too far gone. It was a really fast-moving fire."

The Fireman turned off the TV with an abrupt movement. His stomach churned. It was one thing to get a little revenge on Maui Sugar, burn some fields, enjoy letting the Bitch out to play. It was another to try to burn a family of cops and firefighters in their home.

They were cops!

"Oh God, help me!" The Fireman stood up, the enormity of the trouble he was in hitting him. He ran to the bathroom and retched over the toilet, but nothing came up. He'd been too keyed up to eat.

And now the blackmailer wanted him to go after them again.

THE MORNING DRAGGED FOR STEVENS. He entertained Kiet, fixed his bottle, and called the insurance company to get the claim going. After Wayne returned, he fell asleep, tanked up on pain medication.

He woke in the afternoon, alarmed that Lei still hadn't arrived. He tried her phone repeatedly, but she never answered. Finally, sick of sitting and watching the driveway, he called South Hilo Station and asked for the chief.

Ohale responded. "No, haven't seen Lei today. She was here until late last night, though, working that vice case, doing computer research. My two detectives had a message from her; they were going to do some interviews today. But now she's not answering her phone."

Stevens couldn't act casual. "Our house was burned down last night. She said she'd come home as soon as she could, and she hasn't."

Exclamations from the chief and explanations from Stevens

about the house. Finally, a long silence from Bruce Ohale. "You worried?"

"Hell yes!" Stevens found himself shouting. "My wife's missing and someone's trying to kill us!"

"I'll put some guys on this right away," Ohale said. "Did she say where she was staying?"

"No. Said it was a fleabag—that's all."

"That could describe half the motels in Hilo, and I'm sorry to say I didn't ask her, either. How about her rental car?"

"I never heard. We had a little communication gap. Sorry I don't have more for you to go on."

"Her phone. We can track her that way."

"No, she said it was on the fritz and she turned it off. Was using a burner."

Another long silence as they both mulled this over. "Seems like she might have been going off the grid," Ohale said.

"I've been concerned this whole time that she was really on the Big Island to go after the Changs herself," Stevens said, every word feeling like a lead weight as it fell from his lips. "I told her our house was burned and we barely got out alive this morning. We have confirmation it was the shroud killer, too." He told Ohale more details about the attack.

"I'll put the detectives she was working with on finding her, and we'll start by checking on Chang's residence right away. We'll let you know," Ohale promised. "I'm putting an APB out on her as a missing person. Take it easy, Stevens. We'll find her. She's smart and a survivor, and she's pregnant. She's not going to take undue risks."

"I hope so." Stevens found himself echoing Pono's earlier sentiment as he hung up.

Wayne had put the baby down for a nap and came out of the back room. Stevens didn't want to alarm him further. "I have to go into the station and take care of some things," Stevens said, easing a pair of Wayne's large house slippers over his burned feet.

"What! You can't go in today, man! You're barely off oxygen!"

"I have to. Got a lead on the arsonist," he lied. "You gonna be okay here by yourself?"

"I guess I'll have to be. Don't know where the heck Lei is," he grumbled. "She should be here by now."

"I know. I'm going to check on that, too," Stevens said, wincing as he eased a shirt down over his head.

"Mike. I don't know if you realize this, but half your hair is gone and your face is blistered. You look like hell."

"I need to do something to catch this guy." Stevens rested his hand on his father-in-law's shoulder. "I have a spare weapon in my truck. I'm going to leave it with you, and I'm sending Jared over here when he gets off work."

"I can handle myself." Wayne flourished one of the steak knives, a light in his eye Stevens knew he would never want to encounter in a dark alley.

"Still. Come with me and I'll give you the gun."

Haggling out at the truck, Stevens ended up taking the smaller ankle rig he kept locked up for raids and leaving Wayne with his regular weapon. As he drove out of the property, every movement painful, his throat still throbbing, he used the phone Wayne had bought him to call Jared, leaving a message for his younger brother to go keep Wayne company at the cottage. He then called Ferreira.

"Boss! What's going on? I saw the news!" the older detective exclaimed.

"I'm coming in. I think our arsonist may be the same one who has been starting the cane fires." He told Ferreira why. "My wife is missing on the Big Island. I can't leave Maui without an ID, and mine was burned."

"I'll call the DMV and get them moving on making you another one," Ferreira said. "Consider it done."

"Well, while I'm waiting for that, let's work the case. We think the arsonist who burned our house could be the same guy." He told Ferreira about the fuel mixture.

"I have been working the case. Eliminated most of my list today, but we still have yours, and some places to go by, like that guy in Happy Valley who wasn't home."

"Let's start there. I want to get this arsonist." Stevens hung up and pressed harder on the gas, ignoring his sore foot.

LEI CALLED Sophie Ang from her car, following Terence Chang in his black Tacoma down a winding, isolated jungle road.

"Sophie, I can't talk long, but I need you to check on the whereabouts of a man named Ray Solomon and a woman named Anela Chang. They're somewhere on the Big Island. Anything you can find out, starting with a physical address. It's urgent."

Sophie's voice was taut with tension. "What are you up to, Lei?"

"I'm following a lead on the shroud killer. I need some intel that's not filtered through the local PD," Lei said, driving with one hand and keeping Chang in sight. He was driving slowly, within the speed limit, no doubt to keep both of them from being pulled over by any random speed traps, notorious on this stretch of quiet road leading out of Hilo.

"I can work that in."

"I need it...like, now," Lei said. "It's critical."

"I'm at the FBI in the middle of a workday," Sophie snapped. "I need a little more to go on from you to drop everything."

"We had another attempt on our lives," Lei said. She couldn't keep the tremble out of her voice as she told Sophie about the fire on Maui last night. "I'm over here on Big Island, and I'm trying to find out who's behind this."

"Okay, I'll get on it right now." Lei could hear the rattle of the woman's keyboard as those long golden-brown fingers went to work. "I have them up. Both have records."

"I know all about that. I just need to know where they are. Physical address."

More rattling.

"I don't have that. Neither of them have driver's licenses. All I have is a PO box in Hilo." She read it off.

"So how about business addresses associated with them?" The farther Lei got from Hilo, the more nervous she became, following Chang into the wilderness. In his living room, he'd offered to help, to show her where Ray and Anela's compound was, and that had made sense. "You'll never find it by yourself," he'd said.

Now Lei was having second thoughts. Chang could be leading her into a trap.

Lei slowed down further, glancing around at the trackless wilderness they were passing through. The Big Island was full of hidden roads and so much jungle it would be no problem to hide her car—and her body.

She wished she'd returned Stevens's calls, but she hadn't wanted him trying to stop her.

"Hmmm," Sophie said. "This is interesting. I see the two of them listed on the board of directors of Paradise Production Enterprises, LTD. There's a physical address listed for that." She rattled off a Hilo address, and Lei committed it to memory.

"So tell me more about what you're doing. Let me help."

"I can't. But I need you to look for the guy who burned our house on Maui if you can." She told Sophie about the message Stevens had left her that the fuel mixture was the same for the cane burns as for their arson attack. "I know it's not a lot to go on. The guys are doing canvassing of Maui Sugar employees and so on, but I don't think anyone has done a search for online connections to this firebug. Can you look for all you can on these two suspects and on this Maui arsonist? I want him strung up—he burned my house and almost took out my family." Lei found her voice thickening. "I have to keep doing what I'm doing over here. Call Stevens at his station with anything you find." She hung up abruptly, afraid she was going to say too much.

Lei refocused on the deserted, winding, two-lane road, ignoring the phone, buzzing like an angry bumblebee on the seat beside her.

There was zero visibility ahead with the choking trees. She sped up and got the Tacoma back in her sights.

The phone was her lifeline. She had to be able to contact Hilo PD when and if she needed to call for backup—but she couldn't call them too soon and have them try to stop her and Chang.

Where was Terence Chang leading her? Chang had said Anela and Ray had a compound out in "the sticks," and it appeared he wasn't exaggerating, even by Big Island–isolation standards. Lei watched her reception bars anxiously as the huge albizia trees, draped in choking veils of vines, leaned over the road to close them into a dim tunnel of green-lit jungle.

CHAPTER TWELVE

THE FIREMAN BUNDLED his clothing into a suitcase and scooped items off his dresser: a comb, a wooden box with the few keepsakes he had from his mother, his class ring, a worn Bible. He'd decided what to do.

It was time to start over. He had cash, and right now no one was looking for him—except for the blackmailer. He could get lost in the crowds on Oahu easily. Having made up his mind, he was galvanized into action. The decision had settled his stomach.

The first thing he'd done was ditch all of his fire-setting equipment and any evidence tying him to the fires. That had been easy to do, dumping the gas and diesel cans, plastic bin, and other items into the Dumpsters behind the mall, burning the receipts.

He'd gone to Ross and bought a cheap suitcase. As he packed, he felt a lightening in his soul.

He had a chance to start a new life. He could buy a new identity on Oahu—someone, somewhere, made fake IDs—and with this cash, he had a cushion to figure out what to do next. He looked around the tattered apartment, regretting that he'd bought the flat screen TV. He couldn't take that with him.

The doorbell buzzed, and he dropped a handful of T-shirts in surprise.

"Shit," he muttered, picking them up. Doorbell had rung more in the last few days than it had the entire time he'd lived in the apartment. His hands were shaking.

Truth was, he was afraid the blackmailer was observing him and knew he was fleeing. Now that he'd seen how thoroughly the cops had been watched in their home, he no longer believed the windows were how he'd been observed.

He still had the tranq gun. It was his only weapon.

He picked it up and went to the door, applied his eye. Two men stood out there, but in the distortion of the fish-eye lens he couldn't recognize them.

"Yes?"

"Kenny Rice?" One of them, a burly looking older man, spoke. "This is the MPD. We need to ask you a few questions."

The Fireman stepped back from the door, his heart rate galloping. They were onto him somehow! What to do? He looked around wildly, but the window was three floors up and there was no fire escape.

He'd have to brazen it out.

"This isn't a good time. I'm sick." His voice wobbled authentically. He felt his heart doing flip-flops like a gaffed fish.

"We're sorry for the inconvenience, sir, but this is important." The man's voice was implacable. "You can answer the questions here, or come down to the station."

The Fireman felt his heart give a sort of squeeze, and then it felt like a giant hand clamped over it, as if wringing out a sponge. Agonizing pain filled his chest, radiating down his arm, dimming his vision.

"Help," he gasped, and was only able to undo the dead bolt before he was swamped in a red wave of agony. His vision wicked out.

Ferreira looked at Stevens as they heard a muffled cry and the thump of a falling body on the other side of the door.

"Kenny? Kenny Rice?" Ferreira yelled, and pounded on the door again. "Something's wrong in there. Maybe someone has him."

"Exigent circumstances enough for me," Stevens said. "You do the honors; my foot's still sore."

Ferreira stepped back and aimed a kick just under the doorknob. The door buckled but held. Another kick and it gave from the jamb, but wouldn't open—there was a body blocking it.

Ferreira applied his shoulder and some heave, and the body slid inward enough for them to see that it belonged to a thin, middle-aged man of medium height, his skin dusky-white, his eyes closed. A gash on his forehead bled sluggishly.

Stevens had his weapon out. He stepped over the body, checking the adjacent room and bathroom. "Clear. He's alone."

"Choking, poison, or heart attack," Ferreira surmised, kneeling beside the man and feeling for a pulse. Stevens called for an ambulance as Ferreira checked the airway, and grimacing, began CPR.

"I'll take a turn when you get tired," Stevens said. "Having a look around." He snapped on gloves he pulled from a back pocket and, in the bedroom, observed the signs of packing. "This guy was leaving in a hurry." He picked up a printed schedule lying in the printer. "This afternoon, in fact." He rifled through the mound of items beside the suitcase and looked inside a pillowcase filled with lumpy items. "Oh yeah. Something going on here." He returned to the other room, holding the pillowcase open. "Check this out."

Ferreira paused his chest compressions. "That's a lotta cash."

They heard the wail of the siren off in the distance. Stevens propped open the broken door, shooing some lookie-loos from the hallway. "He's having a medical emergency. Help is on the way." Reluctantly, the doors closed, but Stevens knew the neighbors would be back to see what they could glean—this was that kind of apartment building. "We'd better take this money down to the station for safekeeping now that we've broken his place wide open." He glanced around. "There doesn't appear to be anything else worth much in here except for that flat screen. I'll get his wallet, too." He gathered the man's things and then relieved Ferreira doing the chest compressions until the medical team arrived.

After Kenny Rice was taken away, Stevens conferred with Ferreira. "I think we should search this place thoroughly for anything connecting Rice with the fires. I mean, this guy is supposed to be broke, on unemployment. So what's he doing with a pillowcase full of cash? And then he's packing with a one-way ticket to Oahu and has a heart attack when we come to the door. Something smells."

"Agree," Ferreira said, mopping his forehead. Sweat rings darkened his navy blue golf shirt.

"Okay, I'm getting a search warrant." Stevens worked his phone for a while, getting one faxed down, and it wasn't long before they were thoroughly searching the premises.

Stevens, in need of a physical break, sat down at the man's computer.

The Internet cookies cache had been wiped. "Dammit," Stevens muttered. As he sat on the plastic office chair up against a counter the man had used for a desk, he looked around at the depressing space: bare, scuffed walls, a parking-lot view obscured by broken blinds, a stolen stop sign in the window, a dirty, old tweed couch.

Yet this man owned more personal things than Stevens did right now. "Insurance is going to come through," Stevens muttered to himself. "It better." He was worried there might be something in the fine print excluding arson.

Sitting there, scrolling through the files on the computer, Stevens's mind returned to Lei for the hundredth time. He'd been grateful for activity to keep his mind off her disappearance. The DMV had completed his ID, but he hadn't been able to get a flight out until four o'clock. It was now one p.m. He'd need to get to the airport soon.

His anger with Lei was on a slow boil, tamped down by worry—

but he knew, once he knew she was safe, he'd feel the full flame of it, and he had no intention of sheltering her from the blast.

"Hey." Ferreira, sifting through the trash, held up a brown UPS box. "This came today. This morning. I wonder what was inside." He looked into the sink, held up a bit of burned paper. "The guy went to some trouble to get rid of whatever this was. Burned it."

Stevens stood up. "If he was the firebug, he probably has a place he stashes all his fire stuff."

They hurried through the cupboards and closet, but found nothing but a barbecue lighter. "He must have ditched anything linking him to the fires." Stevens flicked the lighter. "This works. I'll take it in."

Just then Ferreira's phone buzzed. He took the call and looked up at Stevens. "FBI patch-through from Oahu for you. Agent Ang."

Stevens took the phone. "Sophie?"

"Hi. Lei asked me to call you with this. I found a guy on some of these arson and firebug forums. I have a computer IP address."

"You've heard from Lei? Is she okay?" He knew he sounded alarmed.

A long pause as Sophie Ang took in his tone. "I think so. She was in a hurry, said it was urgent. Wanted me to run some background on some people and search for this Maui arsonist. She told me to call you if I found a lead."

"When was this? Did she say where she was? What she was doing?" He fired the questions like bullets.

"Just said that she was on the Big Island, chasing down some leads. She called me maybe an hour ago."

She wasn't kidnapped. She's gone rogue. Just as he'd suspected.

Stevens controlled his voice with an effort. "Great. Thanks for this. We are closing in on this guy, and this might make all the difference. Who were the suspects Lei wanted you to find?"

"Anela Chang and Ray Solomon."

Stevens's stomach dropped. Those two names were a little piece of ancient history he'd rather never hear again. "Did she say why she wanted the address?"

"I assume to go roust them. As I said, she was on the road."

"Thanks, Sophie." Stevens hung up before he said anything more and unplugged the computer. "Taking this in for evidence. Rice didn't leave much physical evidence, but we may get him with his online footprint. And now I have a few calls to make." He speed-dialed Captain Ohale on the Big Island.

LEI PULLED OVER BEHIND CHANG, where he'd pulled his vehicle into a long driveway off the main road. He turned off the driveway and pulled the truck up under some trees. It wasn't hidden, but it wasn't obvious, either. Lei pulled her battered rental in beside his. They got out. Lei kept her hands loose, assuring easy access to her weapon.

"So. Where's this compound?"

"I didn't want to alert them to us. They know my truck. It's down the main road a bit farther. We could do a drive-by in your car and then park again. I'm still not sure how you plan to go about this," Chang said. His olive complexion looked pale.

"Me neither," Lei said, frowning. "But I need your help. The enemy of my enemy is my friend, remember?"

"I said I'd show you where it was—that's all." Chang tightened his jaw.

"Okay, then. I need to see exactly where it is before you take off."

Without another word, he got into her car. Lei sucked in a breath, hoping she was even somewhat in the ballpark of doing the right thing, and got in beside him.

"Pull back onto the main road," Chang said. "We'll drive by the entrance. Then you can come back here and park. I think they have surveillance cams at the turnoff, which is why I didn't want to take my truck past it."

Silently now, they drove back onto the main road, and finally, Chang pointed down a side road, a red-dirt slash in the jungle. "It's down there."

Lei drove by at a sedate pace, peering down the road. "I can't see anything."

"You wouldn't be able to. They're trying to stay under the radar."

Lei drove a while before she found a pullout to use to turn the car around, then made her way back. This situation was looking pretty impossible right now. Her brain scrambled for a solution.

She parked next to Chang's truck again. "Now, what can you tell me about the compound? I need to know what I'm getting into."

"I thought of that." Chang reached inside the light khaki Windbreaker he wore over a shoulder rig with a Beretta holstered in it. Lei tensed, her hand near her weapon, but he only drew out a small tablet computer. "I can draw you a map." Using a stylus, he drew a rectangular compound. "Ten-foot fence around the compound with razor wire around the top. Bulletproof gatehouse at the entrance. At least six armed guards. A bunkhouse in back. This is all to guard the meth lab and distribution facilities back there."

Lei felt her belly tighten. This compound was no place to take on by herself. "So you mean for me to drop you off and then take on armed men in a fenced compound by myself?" Lei snorted. "I'm crazy, but I'm not stupid."

Chang shrugged. "Not my problem."

So Chang wouldn't help, but she could call in a raid if she had probable cause, which she did with Chang as a witness. She whipped out her weapon and pointed it at Chang.

"Put your hands on the dashboard."

Chang narrowed his eyes. "This is how you thank me?"

"For all I know, you're lying out your ass and sending me on a wild-goose chase, or into a trap. You're my bird in the hand right now. One dead Chang or another, it makes no difference to me." Lei spat the words harshly, hoping he wasn't going to call her bluff.

Chang put his hands on the dash. "I can't believe I helped you."

Lei pulled handcuffs out of her back pocket, keeping the weapon on him. She snapped one on his wrist, slid the other through the handle of the door, and then cuffed his other wrist. She removed the Beretta and rifled his pockets. She took out a switchblade and put the items in the backseat. She tweaked up his pant leg, and sure enough, he was wearing an ankle holster, too. She reached down and pulled the weapon out. "Sorry about this, Terence. It's for your own protection."

"Really." Anger stained Chang's cheeks, the tops of his ears. "I'm not going to forget this, Texeira."

"You were going straight, right? So go straight." She took out her phone and called Ohale, getting out of the car to keep out of Chang's hearing range. "Captain? This is Lei Texeira. I have some reliable intel on busting a serious meth lab."

She endured the captain's rant about the trouble she'd caused and felt her throat tighten as he told her how Stevens had called her in as a missing person. "I'll get SWAT mustered out on this, but if this raid is a dud, I'll have your badge myself," Ohale barked, hanging up so hard she recoiled from the sound.

It was time to call Stevens. He picked up right away, his voice raspy and ragged.

"Lei! My God, where are you?"

"I'm okay. I'm on the shroud killer," Lei said. Hearing Stevens's voice made tears well up. "You have to understand. I'm going to make them stop coming after us."

"Lei! No, dammit! The chief's got his men looking for you!"

"I just talked to Ohale. It's not the Chang we thought it was, and we're going in with SWAT to raid the place." She kept her voice as flat and uninflected as she could. "It's not Terence Chang behind the attacks—it's been Ray Solomon and Anela. They took over the family business, not Terence, which is why Sophie never could find anything on him. Anyway, I don't expect you to agree with what I've done. We can work this all out later when they're in custody. I love you." She hung up, turning off the ringer.

She knew she was burning him right now.

Burning the trust and companionship they'd built.

Burning the love between them.

But Lei had decided she would worry about fixing her marriage when she'd stopped their real enemy—because none of it mattered as long as the shroud killer was after them.

CHAPTER THIRTEEN

STEVENS PICKED UP HIS WEAPON, checked separately, and duffel bag and strode out of the Hilo Airport. Captain Ohale was leaning on his beefed-up police SUV. A line separated his brows, and Oakleys hid his eyes as Stevens arrived at the curb.

"You look like hell, man," Ohale said. "Sure you're up to this?"

"I've been through hell, and pissed as hell is what I am," Stevens said. "Just a little singed around the edges." He kept forgetting his burns were so obvious—being back on the job had kept his mind off it.

"We're on our way out to the meth lab location," Ohale said. "I've got Kevlar in the back for you and some extra weapons."

"Thanks for picking me up." Stevens tossed his bag into the backseat and picked up the vest. He got in beside the burly chief. "So you heard from Lei? She told me she called you."

"This intel better be legit. I'm serious. I've got full SWAT gathered from all over the island. They're meeting Lei at a checkpoint near the Chang compound, which is way out in the jungle." The chief put on his siren and lights to get through the backed-up traffic of downtown Hilo. "If it turns out to be bogus and not the big operation she says it is, I'm going to be the first in line to take away your wife's badge."

"I'll be right behind you," Stevens said. He bit down on all the rest he wanted to say. None of it would help the situation, which hopefully, was coming to a head and soon would be resolved. He checked in with himself on that. If Lei was right and these Changs were the culprits behind the shrouds, was he going to feel better about Lei taking off without him?

No. No, he wasn't. Not just because she hadn't trusted him enough to tell him what she was up to, but also because she'd put herself in danger even as she'd excluded him. He felt a vicious satisfaction that he was going to be there at the takedown of the shroud killer anyway.

They blazed through Hilo's run-down urban sprawl and distinctive banyan-tree-lined harbor and into the outskirts, Ohale getting updates on the radio periodically.

They drove and drove, down a winding two-lane asphalt road through overhanging jungle. The area had an oppressive, steamy feel, and not a breath of wind stirred huge trees trailing draped vines over the road. Stevens thought of Lei coming out here alone, hunting these dangerous gangsters, and that steel band of anger and fear tightened even further.

Ohale finally whipped a right turn onto a tiny road that broke the monotony of the jungle. Stevens was pretty sure if he'd been driving, he would have missed it. Ohale plowed the SUV into the bushes beside several other similar vehicles. The SWAT team was gathering on the road. They had set up sawhorse barriers to keep anyone from coming in or out.

Stevens's heart sped up. Finally. Lei was here.

And sure enough, as he got out of the SUV, he heard a door slam and there she was, wearing an oversized Kevlar vest that came to the bottom of her hips, her face tense and so pale that the little freckles stood out like flecks of nutmeg on cream, her wild curls trapped into a rubber-banded ball on the back of her head.

She'd never looked more beautiful.

He wanted to grab her and smash her against him and kiss her into submission, and when he had her where he wanted her, he'd put her over his knee and spank that ass until she cried. Instead he stared her down without a word, feeling the anger he'd been battling swell in his chest and shoot out of his eyes.

Lei blinked tear-filled brown eyes, pleading with him. Her full mouth trembled. "I did it for us. For our family."

Ohale broke the spell, stomping around the vehicle to grab Lei's arm. "You two can have your domestic spat after the raid. Texeira, we need intel. Come over here." He hauled her, still gazing back at Stevens, over to the SWAT leader.

Stevens blinked to refocus himself, breathing deeply through his nose as he watched his wife. She oriented herself in front of the map spread out on the hood of one of the SUVs.

"Give me a pen." Someone handed her a Sharpie, and she drew a rough rectangle down a thread of road on the map. "I have the witness in the car who told me about the compound. Let me get him." She hurried back to the rental car and opened the passenger door. Stevens's eyes widened as he saw that it was Terence Chang cuffed to the door. The young man's face twisted with anger.

"Screw you, Texeira," Chang spat. "You have no right to hold me."

Lei ignored this and unlocked one side of the cuffs, then grabbed Chang by the hair and hauled him out of the car. Stevens felt one side of his mouth pull up in a reluctant smile as she thrust the man over to the SWAT team.

Lei was just so badass. God, she pissed him off—and still she impressed him. Was their relationship ever going to be simple? He was pretty sure it wasn't.

"I'm not helping you," Chang said. "I demand to speak to a lawyer."

"You're not being charged with anything," Ohale said. "You're a witness. That's all, at this point."

Lei had gone back to the car, and this time she brought an electronic tablet over. "He drew a diagram on this."

The team conferred over the tablet, peppering Chang with questions. At some point the young man decided it was in his best interest to cooperate and potentially get his cousins neutralized, because soon he was drawing on the map and showing them what he knew about the compound. Finally, he said, "That's all I know."

Ohale looked at Lei. "You two are staying here until the raid's over. You can stow him in the back of my SUV, and we'll formalize his statement back at the station after the raid."

"Captain, I'm going on the raid. I'm the one who brought you in!" Lei exclaimed, a flush sweeping up her neck to stain her cheeks with red, that blush Stevens knew she hated. "I deserve to be there!"

"You've been ordered by the FBI not to have anything to do with the Changs, and I can't allow your presence to taint our case," Ohale said. "Take the witness to my vehicle, guard him, and wait until we get back. You've done more than enough today."

Stevens felt that satisfaction again. *That will fix her wagon, dammit.* He caught Ohale's eye and gave a tiny nod of thanks, but the captain pretended not to see it.

"Saddle up, everyone. Get all the weapons you can carry and plenty of extra ammo," the SWAT leader said. "We're breaking into three teams. Lieutenant Stevens, Captain Ohale, you're with Sergeant George here. We'll approach from three directions and generate some shock and awe."

Stevens saw Lei give Chang's arm an angry tug as she led the man back to the captain's SUV with its grilled, prisoner-holding backseat.

Good. She'll be safe. That's all that really matters.

Stevens gave his full attention to the SWAT leader and the plan of attack.

Lei stuffed Terence Chang into the back of Ohale's SUV. As she did so, she spotted Stevens's duffel bag on the seat. She pulled it out and tossed it in the passenger-side front seat.

"Hey. Can I at least be cuffed in front? He said I'm not being charged with anything," Chang said.

Lei turned Chang around and put the cuffs back on, looser this time.

"Seems like a lot of manpower and gun power." He licked his lips nervously. "Think it's going to be enough?"

"I'm not discussing it with you. Get in. I'll roll the windows down."

Chang complied.

Lei busied herself with shutting the door and making sure it was locked before she returned to Ohale's side.

"Captain. Can I get your keys?" she whispered so as not to interrupt the SWAT leader's planning. Ohale dug them out of his pocket without looking at her and slapped them into her hand. Lei couldn't help looking over at Stevens.

He was standing tall, his legs braced wide, arms crossed on his chest, eyes intent on the SWAT leader. Even as conflicted as she was, the sight of him took her breath away.

But it was like she'd ceased to exist for him. Her heart felt bruised at the anger she'd seen in his flame-burned face. Her gaze drifted over the injured side of his head. His dark hair was scorched down to stubble, his cheek and square jaw blistered. She could see more red marks on his arms, and his hands were covered in black leather shooting gloves, probably to protect burns on his hands.

Lei felt herself frowning as she turned and went back to the SUV.

Stevens couldn't be that badly injured if he was here, participating in the raid, but she couldn't wait to get his clothes off and inspect the damage.

That was if he let her get close to him again.

Making her stay back—it was all a male conspiracy. Ohale was holding her back because she was pregnant. They were all in it together, the bastards. She balled her fists, realized she was more embarrassed than angry, humiliated by Ohale's words to her in front of the men, humiliated by Stevens refusing to speak to her.

Ohale had a reasonable objection, though. Her involvement could provide defense attorneys with arguing points.

The situation was out of her hands, so she'd have to make the best of it. After they left, she could set up a sniper station and watch the road, at least.

Lei went around to the back of the SUV and hit the button, releasing the hatch. "Thought you were going to roll down the windows. It's getting hot in here," Chang complained.

"All in good time," Lei said, picking up a sharpshooter rifle from the pile of weaponry in back, along with an extra weapon. She stowed the pistol in her belt.

Stevens appeared. "What are you doing?" His voice was rough and gravelly. "I heard the captain tell you to stay back and guard the witness."

"This is me staying back and guarding the witness," Lei said, trying for neutral.

Ohale appeared on the other side. "You can keep the sniper rifle and watch the road," he said. "But don't leave the witness. We need him alive."

"Gee, thanks," Chang piped up from the backseat. "Your concern is touching."

Stevens narrowed his eyes but didn't say anything further, instead picking up a second pistol and a hip holster ringed in ammo loops, along with a pump-action shotgun and a handful of tear-gas grenades.

Lei took her time loading the sniper rifle with copper-jacketed long-distance ammo, watching Stevens out of the corner of her eye. He rammed shotgun shells into the loops around the belt holster, then slung it around his waist and cranked the buckle.

She wished the sight didn't do something melty to her insides, but it did. He was a warrior, girding for battle, and she just wanted to be at his side.

Beside him, Ohale was almost done loading up. The station chief looked downright intimidating, especially once he pulled a black-visor helmet out of the back and put it on, handing another one to Stevens.

Lei slid another shell into the loader, ratcheted it in. Held up the gun, sighted through the viewfinder down the road, thinking back to her FBI sniper training. She'd done well at distance shooting and was glad to feel the familiar heft of the steel in her arms. It was a good distraction.

"Glad to see you wearing a vest, at least." Stevens sliced narrowed blue eyes at her, the black helmet under his arm. He was referring to the baby, she knew. Lei ignored this, busying herself with her weapon as he loaded the last of the shotgun shells in his belt and then stowed the grenades in pockets on his vest.

"Moving out!" the commander said from up ahead. "Helmets and comms on!"

Ohale brushed past Lei, striding off.

Lei felt rather than saw Stevens, suddenly beside her. Felt his gloved hand grab her chin, tilting her head up. Felt his mouth brand hers in a hard, hot kiss that instantly overwhelmed her and promised all the retribution she had coming.

That kiss was contradicted by the gentle touch of his hand on her cheek as his lips left hers. Her eyes were closed, blinded by instant tears. He spun away, clapping the sleek black helmet on and disappearing down the road at a jog with the rest of the men.

"Touching," Chang said. "Mind rolling down the windows?"

Lei forced her legs to work, walking around to the front of the SUV. She leaned the sniper rifle on the fender and opened the door, inserting the key to roll down the windows. Damn, that man was her personal kryptonite.

She wondered, feeling the tightness of fear for the team as they disappeared down the road, if that was what she was for him, too.

CHAPTER FOURTEEN

THE FIREMAN WOKE up by degrees, awareness dawning with the red light he began to be able to process behind his eyes.

He was aware of a terrible weariness. Breathing was an effort. He tried to open his eyes, but they seemed to be gummed shut, and that sent a spike of panic shooting to his heart. That overworked organ responded with that familiar flip-flopping sensation. This time that sensation triggered an alarm, and the Fireman heard people responding to the shrill beeping with a bustle and murmur of voices. Seconds later, he felt something warm and energizing stabilize his heart rate as medication hit his system.

Medication. He must be in a hospital.

"My eyes won't open," he muttered.

"Oh, let me help you with that." Some sort of wetness on his eyes, and then, blinking, he was able to open them. He looked around blearily. He was in a hospital bed, and two nurses were beside him, one on either side. They were watching the heart monitor.

There were no flowers. No visitors. There was no one to know or care that he was here. Despair felt like it flowed from his damaged heart down his veins like black poison.

"Did I have a heart attack?" His voice felt wispy.

"Yes, sir, you did. In fact, it's a good thing you woke up. You can discuss the surgery you need with the doctor," one of the nurses said. She was young and pretty, and white teeth almost blinded him when she smiled.

He remembered something bad had been happening when he fell at the door. What was it? "I don't remember how I got here."

"You collapsed in your apartment. Some police officers called it in," she said. "You were so lucky they were there. They kept you alive with CPR until the ambulance came."

Dimly, he remembered now, the mental images as blurred as newspaper with coffee spilled on it.

Packing in his bedroom.

The bell at the door. Two men. Cops.

His heart squeezed again, and on the monitor it bounced like a salmon leaping upstream.

"Cough," the nurse commanded. The Fireman coughed, and the heart line on the monitor settled back to its regular blipping. "You need to avoid stress until you have your operation," the nurse said, and she patted his hand. "If it acts up again, cough and see if you can get it back in rhythm. If not—well, the alarm will bring us. Doctor will be here shortly to tell you about the procedure you need."

The Fireman watched the two nurses leave. They'd turned on the TV, but it was muted. He watched the images move, talk, dance, and change. A meaningless pantomime.

His life was over.

That pillowcase of money had been on his bed, along with his ticket to Oahu. They'd either have left it, in which case it would be stolen—or worse, they'd taken it in as evidence against him.

His heart jerked.

He coughed, and it settled again.

Yes. His life was over. Did he want to live, with prison ahead? His life had already been empty of anything good or lovely, except the Bitch when she was flaming around him in her glory. No. He didn't want to live. Go through a trial. End his pathetic days in a cell.

All he needed was a little stress to finish him off.

He reached over and peeled off the electrodes taped over his heart. The machine whined flatly in protest, but now he was determined. He yanked out the IV running into his hand and sat up, his head swimming. He swung his legs out of the bed, and feeling the first sense of hope he'd had in weeks, he stood up and walked into his destiny.

STEVENS TROTTED with Ohale and the SWAT commander assigned to them down the main road. They'd decided to penetrate the jungle and come at the compound from three sides, but not the front drive with the cameras. Stevens's group was coming from the far right of where they'd been parked.

His breath hissed in the comm, echoing along with Ohale's and that of Sergeant George, a squat, muscular man who set a good pace along the road.

Stevens tried not to think of Lei. The fragility of the bone of her jaw in his hand as he seized it, overcome with the need to touch her one last time. The feel of those lush, full lips, slightly parted in surprise, beneath his. The penetration of his tongue into the silky cavern of her mouth. Instant buckling of her knees as she sagged against him.

She is mine.

Her body responded to him like kindling to flame. What was between them always would be. And then he'd caressed her cheek when he'd meant to be hard and punishing. Because she always undid him that way.

He wasn't sorry for it.

If he died today, he knew she'd never be able to forget him—if the child he'd left her with wasn't enough reminder. Somehow that mattered more than he wanted it to.

The leader made a hand gesture, and they dove into the jungle.

Visibility was tough with the thick brush, dangling vines, and huge overhanging trees casting shadow. Stevens wished he could take the helmet off as sweat pearled down his blistered face, stinging his skin and eyes. His sore throat rasped at his rapid breathing.

The team leader stopped, and Stevens and Ohale pressed close from behind as he took a compass heading. Then, compass held in front of him, they stalked forward, trying to keep from breaking branches and making noise.

Stevens's whole awareness narrowed to following Ohale's bulk, scanning behind them periodically, his shotgun at the ready, as the team leader pushed deeper and deeper into the jungle and they navigated the constant obstacles before and around them.

It seemed to take forever to find their positions. The comms were mostly silent but for brief coded messages. Stevens couldn't see the wall of the compound, which was chain-link wire, from what Chang had said. They stayed pulled back while one of the tech officers tried to assess how many cameras and what other alarm equipment were operating. Chang had thought there were only cameras at the front of the compound, but Stevens knew he'd have been thinking of a break-in from somewhere less reinforced if he were defending the compound.

"Cameras disabled. Move in," crackled the comms, and Stevens and Ohale followed George and reached the ten-foot chain-link barrier, topped with a coil of razor wire as Chang had described.

George and Ohale each unclipped a pair of long-handled wire cutters and went to work on the fence. The snapping of the stout steel wire made the hairs rise on the back of Stevens's neck as he held the shotgun at the ready, covering the other two officers as they made short work of cutting an opening in the barrier.

He scanned inside the compound. No movement in the lazy, hot afternoon sun. The gatehouse, which was manned all day according to Chang, was out of sight of the spot they'd chosen in the deep shadow of an overhanging mango tree. Stevens could see the main house, with its barred and shuttered windows, and could hear the rumble of an air conditioner—keeping it cool inside, but also keeping the suspects unaware of what was going on outside. Stevens heard the clattering chuff of a generator and was grateful for the sound masking it provided.

The bunkhouse was directly in front of them, and they would be visible if anyone looked out the windows. It appeared deserted. A nearby long metal barn thrummed with more air conditioning.

Everyone here was in a building, working away at their criminal tasks.

Stevens felt an uneasy prickling under his armpits.

This was too easy. It could be a trap. What did they know about Terence Chang and his intel, really?

Stevens spotted movement across the compound—a gleam on something dark in the underbrush. The other team, penetrating from that side. It was reassuring to know they were surrounding the place and the plan was to breach the buildings at the same time, unleashing hell on the inhabitants all at once.

The wire fence was open finally, cut in a triangular flap. Stevens went through first, staying bent low, the shotgun in hand at the ready. Each team had been assigned to a building.

His team had the main house.

The three of them trotted low around the outside of the house, well below the windowsills, and Stevens suddenly saw why no one was outside the buildings.

Stevens lifted the shotgun to his shoulder, mouth gone dry at the sight of a huge German shepherd and a Doberman hurtling toward them from the gatehouse.

He was glad the first rounds he'd loaded in the shotgun were rubber "beanbags" as he nailed the German shepherd in the chest. The big dog yelped and flipped in the air, but almost instantly got up off the ground and kept coming. Those bastards had thick coats—part of what made them good guard dogs. Ohale had temporarily disabled the Doberman, and Stevens whipped out a Taser and shot the shepherd with it.

This time the dog stayed down.

All this had given the men in the gatehouse time to respond, and now they were in trouble as two men stood out from the kiosk, automatic weapons in their hands.

Ohale and Stevens retreated full speed back behind the main house as the air erupted in gunfire. "Back entrance!" George barked, and Stevens heard the crash of the back door caving as the sturdy sergeant kicked it in. All around them, Stevens could hear the sounds of every building under simultaneous attack.

He cocked the shotgun again and hurried into the house after George.

There were at least six rooms inside, and it didn't take long to use up all his beanbag ammo. Stevens dropped the shotgun and switched to his police-issue Glock, and all was a blur of action: staccato thudding of bullets, the rasping hiss of his breath in his ears in the helmet, the spin-and-duck of dodging and getting in a shot.

And then he heard the roar of an engine and was unable to do anything more than spot the black silhouette of a big SUV speeding out of the metal barn, tearing down the closed gate as it exited full speed.

Stevens's distraction cost him as he felt himself get hit from behind, a round smacking him in the back so hard he hit the wall and slid down, breath knocked out of his lungs.

Face down on the ground, sucking as hard as he could to get some air into his lungs, he heard the thud of boots approaching. He shut his eyes, bracing for the head shot that would end it all.

"Get up, man." Ohale's voice. A thick hand grabbed his, hauled him upright. "Took a hit to your back, but the vest got it."

Moving seemed to get his diaphragm muscles working again, and he sucked a great ragged, burning lungful of air and coughed wet and hard. He kept coughing as he followed Ohale, still stunned, and wiped his hand across his mouth. Even through the polarized lens of the helmet, he could see a heavy smear of black blood on the back of his hand.

No time to worry about it now.

They moved through the house, flipping over the prisoners and zip-tying them at their hands and feet. George tapped his helmet. "Subjects subdued. Rendezvous at the metal barn."

Stevens, Ohale, and George left the houseful of prisoners and rejoined the rest of the team. The SWAT leader held up a big white bag of powder from a pile on a long steel table. "Looks like the intel on this raid was good."

"Where are Chang and Solomon?" Stevens asked.

"Haven't spotted them yet, but we have a lot of suspects to iden-tify," the SWAT leader said. "Let's bring all the prisoners out."

Stevens felt a terrible suspicion. "Did anyone get an eyeball on who was in that black SUV?"

"Tinted windows, and they blew past just as we were breaching the barn," one of the team members said.

"Lei," Stevens breathed. He turned and ran toward the gatehouse and the road beyond it.

CHAPTER FIFTEEN

Lᴇɪ ᴍᴏᴠᴇᴅ the SUV with Chang in it closer to the top of the road, to a spot she planned to keep in view. She left Chang in the vehicle with the windows cracked, under a tree's shade with a bottle of water—just like when she left Keiki in the car.

She missed her faithful dog. That made her think of her dad and baby Kiet, and as she walked up the narrow road through the humid, deserted jungle, Lei felt a visceral longing for home, for the baby—and remembered with a wrench of her gut that the house was gone.

At least those she loved were still alive, and she was here to keep it that way.

She hiked past the yellow plastic barrier to the main road and looked around for a good vantage point. She eventually picked a spot on the branch of a large mango tree to set up the sniper rifle. The branch wasn't more than ten feet off the ground, but getting up was going to be a little challenging.

Lei slung the rifle over her shoulder with its strap to free her arms, and taking hold of a thick vine, used it to haul herself up into the tree.

Once up, she was surprised at how wide and comfortable the branch was. She stretched out on her belly and opened the tripod already attached to the barrel of the rifle. Sighting down the barrel, she was able to get coverage of the driveway leading into the compound and still see where she'd stashed the SUV.

Now for the waiting.

Lei sighted into the eyepiece, choosing an optimal kill zone for anyone departing the compound. They'd probably be driving, so she clicked the height adjustment a little higher.

She felt something brushing her arm and looked down. Ants were running around in agitation, covering her arm. She'd lain right in the middle of their pathway through the mango tree. "Shit." She brushed the ants off, but more just swirled up to take their place.

This situation was not going to improve if she stayed here. The choice was to endure the ants or move. She decided to endure.

Lying flat on the branch, she felt the pressure on her uterus, and a flutter down there told her Baby didn't like it. "Okay, moving," she muttered, and twisted onto one hip, raising a leg to the side so the pressure was off her pelvis.

The fluttering stopped.

Unfortunately, now she had time to think.

Stevens was obviously mad at her. His silent glare when he first arrived told her he was just waiting for the right time and place to hash things out, and she wasn't looking forward to it—but that kiss he'd left her with told her he still loved her and wanted her to know it, in spite of everything.

In case he doesn't come back.

Lei didn't want to think of that. She wouldn't think of him dead, of what that would look like, a terrible mental picture all too ready to form in her thoughts. Instead, she rehearsed what she'd say when they finally had their showdown.

When this was all over, he'd forgive her, see she'd done what had to be done. But in fully giving herself to him in marriage, she'd made her body his. She knew that now.

If she was ever going to assert herself with him, she'd better not let him touch her.

Lei rested her chin on folded arms, watching the fork of the road into the compound, trying not to imagine every step of the raid. She hadn't listened to the plans just so she wouldn't be tortured thinking about it.

Fifteen minutes passed.

Her eyes grew heavy. It was late afternoon, the witching hour when Baby laid claim and dragged her into an afternoon nap.

Lei shifted position, switching her weight to the other hip, brushing off another several hundred ants. She watched the street, noticing shafts of sunlight falling through the foliage, dust motes spinning through them like pollen. Gradually, as she settled into the natural environment of the jungle, she noticed sounds she'd missed at first. The humming of a dragonfly's wings as it flew by, gold dust tossing in its wake. The longing coo of a dove in search of a mate. A hushing of wind somewhere off in the distance, moving the tops of jungle trees. The cluck of a francolin grouse in the leaves of the forest floor.

Her sensitive nose picked up the undercurrent of moss and mold within the bark of the tree, and she blew out a breath, turning to check on the SUV.

Nothing had moved in the vehicle. Chang was out of sight. He'd probably succumbed to a doze on the backseat.

She hoisted herself upright, sighting again, muscling her body back into awareness.

Nothing.

Thirty minutes passed.

Suddenly, gunfire erupted. It was so loud, so intense and close; Lei's startled jerk almost threw her out of the tree. She gripped the branch with one arm, the other stabilizing the rifle.

Lei could hear the different kinds of weapons shattering the peace of the forest: the short, sharp *bam-bam-bam* of pistols, the heavy *ka-boom!* of a shotgun, the stuttering clatter of automatic fire. Lei could swear she smelled the chemical after-burn smell of weapons' discharge even as she kept her eye to the viewfinder.

She practiced her relaxation breathing: in through the nose, out through the mouth. *In to the count of three, out to the count of five.* Alert, ready to respond, and at ease. She was safe here, high up and out of sight, and the advantage was all hers. There was no way to have a clue what the hell was going on, and the only way she could help was if someone was escaping and she stopped that.

And for that she needed to be calm, focused, and ready to fire.

She heard the vehicle before she saw it, the throaty roar of an eight-cylinder engine under full acceleration. When the shiny black Escalade appeared, almost up on two tires as it tried to make the turn out of the drive onto the main road, it loomed unnaturally large in the viewfinder.

Cliché gangster car. She aimed at the front tire on the driver's side and gently squeezed the trigger.

The recoil smacked her hard enough in the shoulder that she knew she'd have a bruise tomorrow. She ratcheted another bullet into the chamber.

The vehicle didn't slow.

She tracked it and shot the other tire.

This time the tire blew with a satisfying *bam!* and the Escalade wove back and forth, still trying to accelerate out of the turn. Lei ratcheted another round and aimed at the heavily tinted windshield. It was almost too close, so she took the shot without being certain she had a bead on the driver.

In her haste, Lei's eye was too close to the viewfinder and the recoil banged it backward, hitting her eye socket.

"Shit!" Lei exclaimed, pulling away. She was going to have a nasty shiner tomorrow. The rifle, already off balance from the recoil, fell off the branch. Eyes still on her target, Lei saw that the glass of the SUV's windshield had spider webbed but not broken.

It must be bulletproof.

The Escalade was still coming with its husky roar, but now someone put on the brakes directly across from her hiding place.

They must have spotted the rifle falling into the underbrush below the tree.

Lei flattened herself against the wood and whipped out her Glock, extending her arms and stabilizing them on the branch. She fired at the driver's side window.

The glass wouldn't break. *Sucker is bulletproof, too.* The window cracked at the top, and Lei squinted, carefully aiming for the gap even as she spotted the gleam of a weapon and heard its report.

A slug buried itself in the mango tree a few inches away, kicking up shards of bark.

"Lucky shot, asshole," she growled, and fired the rest of the clip at the gap in the window.

The driver must have decided Lei had the advantage because the Escalade lurched forward again, rolling along on flat tires.

Lei was done trying to hit anything through the bulletproof glass. She dropped the Glock and pulled the extra she'd stowed in her belt, aiming at the back tires. She hit one, and it made a satisfying smacking sound as the round punched through the tough rubber—but it wasn't a big enough hole to blow the tire, and the Escalade accelerated on, flapping down the road.

Not going fast—but going.

Lei sat up, holstered her weapon, turned to one side, and slid down from the branch to dangle by her hands, dropping the last three feet into the deep leaf mulch under the tree. She grabbed the fallen sniper rifle and her spent Glock and ran back toward the SUV, already digging Ohale's keys out of her pocket.

Terence Chang was sitting upright, eyes wide with alarm, as Lei beeped open the vehicle and jumped in, cramming in the key and turning it on.

"Let me out," he pleaded. "Gimme a gun. Let me help."

Lei didn't dignify this with an answer as she threw the truck into reverse and then blazed forward, laying down rubber as she made the turn onto the main road. Captain Ohale's vehicle hurtled down the narrow road after the fleeing Escalade.

"Get on the floor," she told Chang, freeing her weapon beside her. She hooked the radio off the dash. "Officer needs assistance! In pursuit of a black Escalade." She named the highway. "Suspects armed and dangerous, escaped compound from SWAT raid."

"Ten-four, Officer. Please identify yourself."

Lei identified herself, driving as fast as she could on the weaving, narrow road.

The Escalade couldn't have gotten that far ahead of her, and yet it seemed it had. She began to wonder if she'd somehow whizzed past it, if they'd ducked off the main road and found a way to hide. She passed a great chunk of cast-off tire, and then another, and finally there was the vehicle, pulled over on bare rims.

Lei came up behind the vehicle and stopped on the shoulder. The smell of hot metal and burned rubber penetrated the SUV, and a bullet burst a halo of cracks in the windshield as they fired on her.

Lei threw herself sideways. Thank God Ohale's vehicle appeared bulletproof too. Lei dropped down below the dash, ramming another clip into her Glock. "Stay down!" she yelled at Chang again.

"No shit!" Chang exclaimed.

Hunched under the steering wheel, Lei considered her options. She didn't want the suspects getting out and fleeing on foot, but sticking her own leg out and getting shot didn't seem like a good idea either.

"We're going to keep them covered and wait for backup," Lei said.

"I'm okay with that," Chang said.

She was starting to like him. She was pretty sure he didn't feel the same.

The minutes seemed to pass like hours. Lei poked her head up periodically to see if anyone was trying to get out of the SUV, but so far, no movement.

Finally, the scream of sirens, and now they were coming from both directions—from Hilo and from the compound.

Some of the SWAT team must be back on the road to respond to her call. Sure enough, one of the SWAT vehicles overshot her spot and spun to face the Escalade. Pulling up behind it, arriving from the other direction, were two regular police cruisers.

The SWAT leader opened his door. Lei spotted Stevens in the passenger side. The leader used a megaphone. "Driver of the Escalade. Put your hands on your head. Get out slowly, and you won't be harmed."

A long moment passed. Then the shattered but unbroken window of the Escalade rolled down. A gun fell out and clattered into the road. "I'm unarmed," a voice called. "But I can't get out."

Lei knew that voice.

She sat up and opened her door, shouting at the SWAT leader, "He's disabled! You have to approach the vehicle and help him out."

No one moved. The SWAT team appeared to be conferring. The police officers had taken defensive positions behind their doors.

This was taking too long, and she wanted to get an eyeball on Ray Solomon herself. Lei darted out from behind her vehicle door and over to the SUV. She couldn't see anyone else through the heavy tinting on the windows, so she slid along the side below the windows' edge as she approached the driver's door, her weapon ready

Lei could see Ray Solomon's face, tense and frowning, his hands on top of his head, reflected in the rearview mirror. She reached him and gave the front door a sudden yank to open it and surprise anyone waiting to take a shot. Ray must have been leaning on the door, because he fell out of the vehicle at her feet, landing on the pavement with a grunt. Folded beside the driver's seat was a wheelchair.

"You," Ray Solomon said, his distinctive golden-brown eyes narrowing on her face.

If it weren't for those eyes, she wouldn't have recognized Ray. The young man she remembered had been handsome and well built; he had taken pride in his body and his ripped muscles.

The man who landed at her feet must have been close to three hundred pounds, his lower body flopping and useless. But she recognized the hate in Ray's eyes from the last time she'd pulled him out of a car. She couldn't help the twist of guilt and regret in her guts, because it was her bullet that had paralyzed him.

The SWAT team surrounded the vehicle, opening the doors. "Clear," the commander said.

"Where's Anela?" Lei asked Ray.

Ray spat. It landed on her jeans-clad leg. "Long gone. Find her yourself."

Lei felt a hand on her arm and knew it was Stevens's. She backed away from Ray as the man was surrounded by the SWAT team, lifted and carried to one of the cruisers. She turned to her husband but didn't have time to speak as Ohale rolled up in another of the SWAT vehicles. He got out and joined them.

"Good work, Lei," the captain said, holding up a neatly wrapped kilo of what looked like crystal methamphetamine. "We have a huge bust here. It was a good raid; no fatalities, thanks to non-lethal ammo."

"Did you get Anela Chang?" Lei knew her voice was high-pitched with anxiety.

Stevens finally spoke. "Wasn't among the prisoners. Thought she'd be in the SUV." His face was grayish, his hair matted to his head with sweat, and Lei frowned at the sight of the red bubbles on his mouth. She reached up. Her fingers came away from his lips bloody.

"You're injured!" she exclaimed. Stevens seemed to deflate all of a sudden, his knees buckling, and he sagged between Lei and Ohale. His breath sounded ragged and wet, and Lei felt panic jolt through her as Ohale caught Stevens and they lowered him to the road.

"First aid is on the way. Think he overdid it back there with his burn injuries, and he took a round to the back of the vest."

"Got something to cover him up with in the back of the truck," Ray yelled from the rolled-down window of the cruiser. "We won't stop coming after you until you're gone."

Lei spun and stomped across the road toward Ray, but Ohale

caught her arm. "Don't let him bait you," he said. "You've done enough. We'll get them all. Don't worry."

"Come and hit me, Texeira," Ray yelled. "Come and hit the man you crippled. You're a dead woman walking, bitch!"

The officer driving the patrol car rolled up the window and pulled away. They heard Ray's muffled shouts for longer than they should have.

Lei knelt next to Stevens. His face was white, his eyes closed, and she heard the fluid bubbling in his lungs as he struggled to breathe. "Where's that ambulance?" she cried, and heard its wail finally approaching.

Several ambulances whizzed by, but only one stopped, as the others continued on to work with the injured at the compound. The emergency team wouldn't let Lei get in as they worked quickly to get an IV into Stevens and put him on oxygen. Lei watched the vehicle pull away, tears blinding her.

"Guess you don't want to see this right now, but at least it's confirmation we've got the right guy." Ohale held up a length of unbleached muslin shroud from a box in the back of the Escalade.

"Something to cover him up with," Lei murmured, repeating Ray's words. *That murdering bastard.*

CHAPTER SIXTEEN

STEVENS never really passed out for any of the horrible hours after he'd collapsed in the road outside of Hilo. He desperately wished he could, just float away into the darkness now that he knew Lei and the baby were safe. But he was stuck in his broken corpse, struggling for every oxygen-enriched breath that he could drag into bruised, burned lungs.

He had ample time to reflect on how he should have stayed at the cottage with Wayne and Kiet and sucked on his oxygen bottle a whole lot longer instead of running off to the Big Island to participate in a raid that would probably have gone down fine without him. In the end, he hadn't been able to do a thing to protect Lei, anyway. Getting out of her car and taking on Solomon in his blacked-out vehicle when none of the SWAT team would even approach?

It's the final straw.

Stevens kept his eyes shut because there was nothing to see in the hospital room but the plastic oxygen tent around him, the usual equipment, and a tiled ceiling ringed with brown circles of damp. They'd shot him up with some sort of painkiller that dulled the panic out of the struggle to breathe, but he was far from any oblivion.

His mind kept circling back to Lei. Sitting beside the SWAT

leader in that vehicle, he'd watched her get out of the car, helpless to do anything as she sidled along the Escalade with her weapon at the ready. He remembered how she peeled the door open and Solomon, who easily could have had a second weapon and plugged her in the head, landed on his back on the pavement and spat on her instead.

It was a feedback loop he couldn't seem to pause. *It's the final straw.*

He didn't even know what that meant, but he felt the truth of it.

He must have fallen into a doze because he woke with a painful gasp to the feel of her hand in his. He knew without glancing down what it looked like: smooth, olive-tan skin; short, pale nails. It was so much smaller than his. A sturdy, capable hand that could handle a gun, a bomb, a dog, a truck, a baby.

Her hands didn't need him for anything.

"Are you awake?" she whispered.

He opened his eyes. His bed was propped at an angle to keep the fluids in his lungs from traveling upward, and she was on the outside of the plastic oxygen tent, a shifting image as if seen through water.

"How are you feeling?"

He shook his head. Speaking hurt too much, but mostly he didn't have anything to say.

"I was so worried." Tears gleamed in her tilted brown eyes, one of them purplish and swollen. Yeah, she was attached to him, all right. Michael Stevens, the man who'd take her shit and keep coming back for more, fool that he was. It didn't mean he had a function in her life beyond sperm donor.

He shut his eyes. Shut her out.

She tightened her hand on his a moment, then withdrew it from beneath the plastic. He heard rustling and scraping and then silence.

A long moment passed.

He cracked his eyelids.

She'd dragged the padded plastic armchair that extended into a bed from the corner and pushed it as close to his bed as possible. Lei was lying on it facing him, hands flat against each other tucked under her cheek, knees drawn up. She had a nasty black eye and scrapes on her arms. Her hair was frizzing out of the ball she'd rubber-banded it into.

She looked dead asleep, her face pale. She'd been so tired since the baby, and today had been intense for everyone.

He wished he could tuck her against him in her special spot, that dip between his collarbone and shoulder. Her head fit perfectly when she lay along his side there, half of a heart he never knew he'd been missing until she filled the space.

Stevens shut his eyes, mad at himself because he knew he breathed easier now that she was beside him.

A cramp woke Lei, a knot in her arm that felt like she'd been punched in that spot. The hospital room was dark but for a fluorescent floor strip and the flashing of small red monitoring lights. Someone had covered her with a blanket, and a paper-covered pillow was tucked between her head and the chair's frame.

Lei looked over at Stevens. He was shrouded in plastic that gleamed faintly in the reflected lights, his face a formless shadow against the white pillows, but she could hear his breathing.

It was steady, regular. Still ragged and a little wet, but more relaxed.

Lei rubbed the charley horse on her arm. It must not have liked all that climbing in and out of the tree. As she rubbed, she thought of the rest of the afternoon after they took Stevens away. Wrapping up at the compound, moving the defendants to holding at the jail. Giving her statement. A post-raid debrief at the station with SWAT. Saying goodbye to Terence Chang as he was held back for more interviews. Turning over her weapons for ballistics tests. Going straight to the hospital the minute Captain Ohale would let her go.

They still hadn't found Anela Chang. Apparently, Ray had let her out of the SUV along the road, because investigators had found a hidden shed with evidence a quad vehicle had been parked there. Fresh tracks led back onto the road and then disappeared.

Anela could be anywhere, probably traveling under a fake ID and trying to get off the island. If she and Ray were as competent and organized as they seemed to be, she'd have assets stashed somewhere.

Lei tried not to let it worry her, but she'd had run-ins before with enemies who just wouldn't give up, and the Changs were the most persistent she'd ever dealt with. She was glad Ohale had assigned a patrol officer, now sitting outside Stevens's room.

Lei needed to touch him. She sneaked her hand up under the plastic tent, scooting to the edge of the chair bed so she could tangle her fingers in his, gently, so as not to wake him.

Her eyes were drifting shut again when she felt his fingers leave hers, and her hand was pushed out. It fell back into her lap.

She sat up, but in the darkness she still couldn't see if his eyes were open. His breathing had changed, though.

"Are you awake?"

No answer.

She lay back down, troubled. He was still mad at her, and she hated that.

It was a long time before she fell back to sleep.

Morning had come, filling the room with moist, rainy Hilo dawn, when Lei next woke. A nurse was working on Stevens, hooking up a cannula for oxygen. Lei watched as she took his vitals, checking his eyes and down his throat, murmuring softly to tell him what she was doing as she worked. Finally, when the oxygen was turned on, the nurse disassembled the tent.

"Oh, you're awake," she said warmly to Lei. "Looks like you could use a shower. You're welcome to use the one in the bathroom."

"Thanks," Lei said. One glance at Stevens's face showed her that his icy blue eyes hadn't thawed. She felt too tired to deal with it at the moment. She went to the bathroom and got into the tiny shower stall. The flow of warmish water felt heavenly, but it was awful to dry off with the tiny, thin towel afterward and have to get back into her filthy clothes. She'd go change at the motel. She wanted to go into the station to listen to Ray Solomon's interview, which she heard was going to be held this morning with his lawyer present.

Dressed, rubbing her dripping hair with the towel, Lei faced Stevens. "I'm going back to the motel and then into the station for a while. I'll be back to see you at lunch."

She waited a long minute. He'd closed his eyes, pretending to be asleep, and didn't answer. She left, her injured eye leaking tears she didn't notice until they wetted her shirt.

CHAPTER SEVENTEEN

Lᴇɪ sᴀᴛ in the observation room at an old Formica counter riddled with cigarette burns from the old days when smoking was allowed. The local DA sat beside her, playing with his phone as he watched the participants gathering. A tinny audio feed piped in the arrival of Ray Solomon, in a wheelchair pushed by his lawyer, a Mainland transplant called Munson. Captain Ohale and one of his detectives, Lono Smith, were conducting the interview. Lei remembered Lono from when she used to work in Hilo. He was still lean and tall but sported a bushy mustache now. He started in.

Lono: "We have your crew in custody. They're eager to make deals, so why don't you be the first and tell us about your operation?"

Solomon: "I don't hear a deal there."

Ohale: "Well, we hear Anela Chang was the brains of your operation. Where is she?"

Solomon: "We're family. I'm not throwing Anela under the bus."

Lono: "We have a witness who will testify Anela was the real boss."

Solomon: "Who's that? They don't know shit."

Munson: "Don't say anything more. We still don't hear a deal here."

Ohale: "We don't have to make a deal, actually. You don't have anything we want but Anela Chang's location. We have all we need to bury you and your operation already."

A long pause. Lei glanced over at the DA. He was a small, dapper Japanese man she'd been briefly introduced to as Tobita. "Going to offer him a deal?" Lei asked.

"We'll see." Tobita shrugged. His eyes still flicked back and forth between the tableau in the interview room and his phone.

Solomon: "I was in charge. Anela is a glorified secretary, though she'd be pissed to hear me say it."

Munson: "Don't say anything more, sir!"

Solomon: "I want to tell them like it is. What the hell, right? So yeah. I took over my dad's operation. My dad, Terry Chang. The real, original Terry Chang, not that lame-ass computer kid living up at the family house."

Lei winced inwardly, thinking how much Terence Chang would hate hearing this. She hoped he never did—it was that kind of comment that might provoke him into criminal action, feeling like he had to prove something. She still remembered the first time she'd met Terence, as an angry teen tagging buildings, then later in a red do-rag, brandishing a .357 Magnum. He'd "gone straight," but she sensed it wouldn't take much to have him resume the family business, and Ray Solomon's taunts could be a trigger.

The interview continued, with Solomon talking in detail on how he ran the business—the meth manufacturing in particular. She perked up and paid attention when Solomon described the gambling operation. This was the case that had originally brought her to the Big Island, and now he was handing it to her on a platter.

"We get protection money from businesses, and my tech department works up profiles on the business owners, figures out what we can tap them for. Then we set up profile-driven gambling to rope them in. It's a low-overhead operation. We have a couple of guys providing muscle and a couple of techies running the games and PayPal accounts. It's a nice, passive income stream."

Lei narrowed her eyes even as she took notes. Plainly, there were going to be some suspects she needed to interview from the people they'd rounded up at the compound—unless that "department" was housed elsewhere.

It was at the disclosure of specifics that Solomon clammed up. "Given you enough for today," he said. "But you can see Anela's role is small."

Lei wondered if he was trying to get the attention off Anela. What could his motivation be? She frowned, concentrating on the physical wreck that was Ray Solomon. He appeared confident and self-contained, even in a prison-orange coverall that barely contained his mass.

"Mr. Solomon has given you more than enough to earn some reduced charges," Munson piped up finally. "What concessions can you give us for information that will actually help this case move forward in court?"

"Let me check with the DA." Ohale got up and picked up the phone off the wall. It buzzed on the counter in front of Tobita.

"I don't have anything to offer him unless he wants to give up Anela Chang," Tobita said. "I'm still not convinced he's the main man."

Lei's estimation of Tobita went up.

Ohale came back and sat at the table. "The DA has nothing to offer you at this time. So far we are charging you with drug manufacturing and trafficking, attempted murder of a police officer, racketeering, and grand larceny."

Solomon's full face reddened and his eyes seemed to swell with rage. Then he tipped his head back and laughed. "Bring it on," he said. "I'm done talking."

They tried a few more times, but Solomon simply turned his wheelchair away from the table. The interview was over.

"I agree with you," Lei said to Tobita. "He's protecting Anela Chang. But why?"

"You'll have to catch her and see," the Japanese man said, stroking his phone with a thumb. "This should be interesting."

"Well, I most likely won't be there to see it," Lei said. "My case is the online gambling on Maui."

"It was good to meet you, then," Tobita said. "Good luck."

Lei waited to go out of the observation room until Solomon and his lawyer had rolled down the hall ahead of her as he was taken back to the local jail. His hearing was going to be tomorrow, and she had no doubt the bail was going to be exorbitant.

Ohale and Lono Smith joined her. "How's Stevens?" Ohale asked.

"He's going to be fine," Lei said. "They told me he'll be discharged this afternoon. Hey, I'm wondering if you rounded up anyone in the raid that seems like the techies he was talking about."

"They didn't exactly have departmental badges on," Ohale said. "But I'll keep you in mind as we sort out the perps and their charges."

They walked down the familiar worn hall into the beehive of cubicles in the main room.

"As long as you prosecute them and the gambling stops on Maui, I'll consider this case closed," Lei said. "We'll be going home tomorrow. Got a baby who needs us, and a house that needs rebuilding. See you, Captain."

He clapped her on the shoulder so that she staggered. "Good to work with you again, Hurricane Lei."

"Haven't heard that one," Lono said. "Got to be a story there."

"Oh, there's a story, all right," Lei said with a grin as she headed for the door. "But I'll let the captain tell it."

The bright bougainvillea and fern trees that decorated the parking lot gave it a tropical feel, but it was what it was: a tired, older area in a bad part of Hilo. She stopped, breathed in the moist, fresh air that smelled uniquely Hilo, and found herself scanning for her silver

Tacoma in the lot out of habit. She'd gone through two of the vehicles since the one she bought here on the Big Island what felt like a dozen years ago.

Lei thought of Dr. Wilson, who lived and worked in Hilo, and wondered if she'd have time for a quick visit with her former therapist—but she didn't want to get into telling that astute woman the situation that existed between her and Stevens. She needed to get back to him at the hospital, anyway.

LEI WISHED she thought he'd be happy to see her.

Stevens hated getting into the wheelchair and having Lei push him down the gleaming linoleum halls of the hospital for checkout late that evening. They'd eaten dinner in the cafeteria. He hoped it was his last hospital meal for a while.

Stevens somehow managed not to speak to her the whole time the doctor had met with them and explained the course of his recovery. He'd been prescribed rest, extra oxygen until the lungs healed enough to process air more effectively, and a course of antibiotics in case of a secondary infection. Follow-up visits to their doctor on Maui had been set up, and now they were heading back to Lei's motel.

He sucked a careful breath through his nose, but it still hurt because the blow to his back from the round during the raid had bruised his already-inflamed lungs. The extreme exertion of running out of the compound had finished him off. SWAT had picked him up, collapsed on the side of the road, out of pity.

All of this was because of Lei.

Hearing her walking behind him, her hands on the wheelchair grips, he had to admit she'd been right. She'd pulled this off. Pushed the envelope all the way out there to find answers and eliminate their enemy while he stayed at home with the baby and barely got out of their burning house alive. Then he'd worked himself over physically and never accomplished a thing to help or protect his wife.

Stevens felt weak. Useless. He wanted to hate her for it. He couldn't quite do that, but he could give her the cold shoulder for a while, even knowing his reaction was childish.

Lei completed the checkout process and sighed as she folded the hospital bill and put it in her pocket. "At least major medical kicked in on this. It was all covered."

He didn't answer.

She pushed the wheelchair through the sliding front doors of the hospital. Out in the entrance, light, blowing rain kissed Stevens's cheeks and tossed the decorative palms in the parking lot. The sun had gone down, and the sky was the black of Tahitian pearl. He smelled that lush, green smell that was Hilo, feeling a pang of nostalgia for his time living here.

"Wait here. I'll bring the car," Lei said.

Stevens didn't obey. He stood slowly, picked up the oxygen canister, and walked down into the parking lot. Lei walked alongside him, glancing up at him with a frown.

"Stubborn. You don't even know where I parked the car." She caught his hand and tugged it. "Over here."

Just getting to the car winded Stevens, and once in the car, he shut his eyes and focused on getting his breath back as she got in her side and started the car. "You're not going to believe what a dive we're in."

He didn't answer. It was all he could do.

She drove them to a cut-rate motel under the banyan trees where she'd been staying. He waited in the car while she went in and paid for another night. The doctor had said he wasn't in shape to deal with going to the airport tonight, and even he knew it.

She came back. "Follow me." She didn't open the door for him or try to help, and he was fiercely glad of it. He didn't want her help.

She unlocked the faded turquoise door of a room on the second floor. A queen-sized bed parked in the middle of the room was covered in a striped, dark spread. A rickety chest of drawers and a plastic-covered armchair with a lamp beside it completed the decor.

"Home sweet home," she said.

"We need another room," Stevens rasped out.

"Why?"

"Need two beds."

"Since when do we need two beds?"

He stepped inside and ignored her, going to the phone. He picked up the handset and dialed for the front desk.

She snatched the handset out of his hand and plunked it down. "I know you're pissed. Say what you've got to say. Let's get this over with."

He picked the phone up, dialed again. "We need a room with two beds," he said to the front desk. Lei huffed out a breath, muttering, and stomped away to pick up and throw her few belongings into her duffel bag.

The front desk directed Stevens to a room a couple doors down. "Door's unlocked. Come pick up the key," the front desk man said. Stevens picked up his bag and the oxygen canister and walked down the hall to the other room.

He was settled on his own double bed, stripped down to a T-shirt and boxers, the TV on, when Lei returned with the key. She set her things down and went into the bathroom.

A minute later he heard the shower running.

He thought of her in there, her face turned up into the warm water. Streams of it flowing down her breasts, which were fuller every time he saw them. Water rippling down the river of her spine, over the dimpled curves of that fantastic ass. Water gushing down those long, strong legs, over her toned arms.

They so seldom got time alone together anymore, and she was in there soaping up all those secret, beautiful crevices without him.

Shit.

Staying mad, staying away from her, was going to be tough.

She didn't make it easier when she came out, a towel wrapped turban-style around her head—but not around her body. He tried to keep his eyes on the TV as she paraded across his line of sight, those unfamiliarly full breasts swaying and begging to be explored, and damn if her flat belly wasn't pooching out, like there was a little round ball down there.

"Come here," he said, muting the TV. "Something's different."

"Something's always different these days," Lei said. "It's so weird. It's like my body just knows what to do." She unwound the towel from her hair, coming to sit beside him naked. "I wanted to show you something—the baby moving. It's been doing it a lot lately."

His legs were straight out on the bed in front of him, and she draped herself across his thighs, propping herself on her elbows across his lap. She must be able to feel how she was affecting him, because her back was over his crotch, but she gave no sign. Instead she took his hand and set it on her smooth, cool belly, on the hard roundness there. "Just keep your hand there for a minute. Baby usually wiggles when I lie on my back."

They both sat there, looking at his hand on her belly.

Redness of his burned skin against the ivory satin of her waist. The sculptured lines of her, from peaked breasts to the round columns of her legs, the dark triangle between. His long fingers, large enough to span the width of her hipbones. The bulge of their child's home beneath the palm of his hand.

He had to remember to breathe, and it was difficult. He told himself it was because his lungs were still bad.

He felt something then, a flutter of movement, a tiny pulse that felt like the tug of a fish on a line. He couldn't stop the widening of his eyes, the grin that lifted his cheeks.

"You play dirty pool, Texeira. I'm still mad at you," he growled, even as he palmed her belly gently, feeling the moth beat of their child's movement. "God, this is amazing."

"I know. She's really in there," Lei breathed. Her smile was luminous, even with her swollen black eye.

"*He. He's* really in there, and he already wants out," Stevens said. His hand stroked her stomach in gentle circles. The baby stopped moving. "Daddy's tucking you in to sleep," Stevens murmured, and then, because he couldn't help it, he leaned over and kissed the place where the flutter of the child's movement had been.

He looked up. Lei's eyes had filled, gazing at him. "You're such an incredible man."

He shut his eyes, feeling his inadequacies. His failure to protect her. Her betrayal in going after their enemy and *not even giving him a chance to go with her.*

"Funny choice of words." He wanted to stop touching her, dump her off his lap, but it felt too incredible to be almost touching his child in her womb. The coolness of her skin had warmed under the circles his hand drew on it. "You don't think much of me if you came here alone to take on Chang." His voice came out thready, weak. Which was how he felt.

"I thought you'd try to stop me."

Now he did push her aside, but gently, moving his knee so she rolled off his lap onto the side of the bed. He crossed his arms over his chest and looked over at the wheezing air conditioner. He didn't want to see her nakedness any longer—it made her seem vulnerable, when he knew she was far from it.

"Of course I would try to stop you. But did it ever occur to you I wanted to get this guy as much as you did?" His voice rose and broke. He began coughing, and now she jumped up and fetched a glass of water from the bathroom and a wad of toilet paper, which she handed him.

He finished coughing and wiped his mouth. Pink smears came away on the paper. He took the water from her, sipped. She went to her suitcase and dressed in sweats and a loose tank shirt. When she came back and sat on the bed beside him, he still noticed her breasts, filling out the shirt, the nipples tight pebbles lifting the fabric. Damn, his libido was a traitor.

"I'm so sorry." Lei sighed, hung her head. Those wild wet curls hung over her face as she covered it with her hands. "I should have...I don't know. Told you my plan. Given you a chance to come with me. But I remembered what you said that day on Haleakala...that you'd turn me in yourself if you needed to, to protect me."

"We should have at least talked about it," he whispered.

"I respect you too much. That's why I couldn't tell you," she whispered back, still not looking at him. "I kept thinking of Anchara. Dying just when she should have been able to meet her son. Physically unable to protect herself. I'm selfish. I didn't want that to happen to me, to you, to our children. I wanted to move on Chang before I was too big to do anything physical."

He shook his head. "We could have figured something out together. And then after the fire? Don't you know I would have moved heaven and earth to protect our family and catch this guy?" He coughed again, and she tried to hand him the water. He waved it away and instead tried to focus on breathing in oxygen through the cannula. "But it turns out I'm glad you were gone. I'm not at all sure we'd have gotten out if Jared hadn't been there, and he was only there because you were away."

"When I heard you on my voicemail telling me about the fire...I don't even know how I ended up at Chang's house. It was just the last straw." Her voice quavered. "I was careful. All the time I was careful. More than I ever used to be."

"You went up to Chang in his house and got him to roll on his family. How was that careful?"

Lei told him how it went down, and he snorted. "Careful? Right. And how about when you got out of your car and got Ray out of the SUV? SWAT wasn't even going in there to get him!"

"I saw his hands on his head. I knew he was disabled, which they didn't, and that he wanted to surrender. I took a small chance there, but I knew things SWAT didn't. About Ray and the kind of man he is." She took a sip of the water in the glass she still held. "He's a bitter coward. I don't think he has the imagination, the brains to be the new Chang leader, no matter what he says." She told him the content of the interview at the station. "We need to find Anela."

"Well, I heard what he said to you, his threats. Whichever of them is running the Chang operation, I think he's the shroud killer. And now he's neutralized."

"That we agree on." She took his hand and lifted it to her lips. He felt the slick lining of her lips as she kissed the exquisitely sensitive, burned tips of his fingers. He tightened involuntarily. "Will you forgive me?"

"I don't think so." He stared at her steadily. "Like you said. That was the last straw."

"Okay. I understand." She went to the bathroom, and he heard the water running as she brushed her teeth, and he thought he might have heard her crying but couldn't be sure. Then the light went out, and her shadow moved across the room. The covers rustled as she got into bed and rustled some more as she turned on her side, away from him.

He lay silently, watching the black shadowy shapes of the banyan tree leaves moving on the outside of the curtains, and he breathed as slowly and as deeply as he could, trying to get oxygen all the way into the bottom of his lungs. Because he had to heal and get stronger and find a way to keep living with this woman.

They had children who needed them.

CHAPTER EIGHTEEN

LEI BARELY REMEMBERED FALLING ASLEEP, and the sun was fully up when she woke with that restless feeling that told her she needed a run.

She swung her legs off the side of the bed and looked over at Stevens. He was still pale, but he was breathing better. She crept in close to lean her head down by his chest, and she didn't hear liquid in his lungs anymore. Still, his color was off, and there were circles under his eyes. He didn't look like he'd slept as well as she had.

He wouldn't miss her if she went out for a quick run. They weren't due at the airport until ten, when they were booked on a puddle jumper back to Maui.

Lei pulled on her shorts, sports bra, and shoes and left a note on the table beside him. She loaded a small can of pepper spray, phone, and her hotel key into her shorts pocket and went out, careful to shut the door quietly behind her.

On the familiar sidewalk buckled by the massive roots of the banyan trees, she breathed a sigh of relief to be moving again. Various aches and pains left over from yesterday's raid reminded her she'd been active the last few days, but it was good to be running at an even pace in her favorite old route, loosening tense muscles by using them.

Lei ran along the edge of the downtown park with its smooth grass and neatly trimmed coconut palms, looking up as a flock of noisy mynahs fluttered past to land on the grass, the flash of their black and white feathers contrasting with their bright yellow beaks, their voices gossipy and loud. The last of the night's coqui frog orchestra gave a few shrill calls from the trees.

Fishermen lined the jetty with their bamboo poles, as they always had. Hilo Bay was smooth as glass, and there was an ever-present gauzy quality to the air from the volcanic emissions from Kilauea Volcano, a constant condition these past years nicknamed "vog." Some people suffered asthma and other breathing problems when it got thick, and Lei was glad it had never bothered her.

She remembered her runs down through town to this park with Keiki, the way her big Rottweiler would lift her nose to sniff the bay and give a little snort as they ran, enjoying the briny smell.

Lei's mind ticked over the argument with Stevens last night, and she felt heaviness bring down her good mood.

He wasn't going to forgive her. At least not right away. Well, she'd give him space while he was recovering, but after that she'd find a way to get them back into bed—because even if he could hold out, she couldn't. She already missed being with him, hated the discord between them even if she knew she deserved it.

Still, it had all worked out. Surely he'd let it go in time.

Lei did some laps around the park, her eyes scanning the faces of pedestrians and commuters, realizing she was still looking for Anela Chang. Of course, there was no sign of the woman. She'd studied the woman's driver's license and memorized her appearance: medium height and weight with a brown, oval face framed in black hair.

She shook her head at herself—Anela was probably long gone. She was getting paranoid. She headed back to the motel, stopping to buy two cups of coffee and a bear claw from a nearby Gas 'N' Go.

Stevens was agitated when she returned to the room, offering him a coffee. He was dressed in pants, but no shirt, and he wasn't wearing the oxygen rig.

"I feel fine," he said when she asked about it. He turned to put on a shirt, and she gasped at the huge purple bruise on the right side of his back.

"Looks bad, does it?" He craned a bit to see. She backed him up so that he could look at it in the mirror. "No wonder it hurts like a sonofabitch."

"Makes me so glad for Kevlar," Lei said. "I hate to even imagine what would have happened to you without it. I'm going to hop in for a quick shower. Want to join me?"

It was worth a try.

She could swear she saw him grit his teeth as he replied. "No."

Lei showered and got dressed for the airport, squashing a little gel into her hair. When she got out he was already dressed, had eaten half the bear claw, and was seated in the cheap plastic armchair, working his phone, with the oxygen back on.

"Got a call from the insurance company. They're going to cover the loss of the house. Unfortunately, not the cost to build a new one —just a flat rate of what the old one was insured for."

"Well, thank God. That's something, right?" Lei whisked a little mascara on her lashes, taking a bite of the pastry to get something in her stomach. "I don't know about you, but I miss Kiet so much. Can't wait to snuggle with him."

"Me too." He stood and picked up his bag. "Let's get on the road."

Lei looked around at the decrepit little room, happy to say goodbye to their first night in separate beds. Hopefully, that wouldn't be an option in her dad's cottage, though it was going to be tight with all of them crammed in there. Still, whatever the sleeping arrangements, she knew she'd rest easier with the shroud killer in custody.

Things had to get better from this point.

Stevens followed Lei onto the tiny aircraft, ducking his head to get in, and took a seat behind her. His long legs brushed the back of her seat, and he felt folded up into the small space, the tin can of a plane tight around him.

They'd gotten to the terminal on time and checked their weapons with the two pilots, who performed everything from stamping tickets to weighing luggage for Ohana Air, an operation that ran a few Cessnas out of the small-aircraft section of Hilo Airport. Neither of them had flown with the outfit before, but Ohana was the only airline with any openings on such short notice.

Stevens tightened his belt and stowed his duffel under his seat. He'd brought the O2 canister but he hadn't wanted to use it unless he had to. Looking around the confined space and knowing how bumpy the wind over the channel between Maui and the Big Island could be, he decided to hook it back up.

A few other passengers bumped past him as he turned on the O2 canister and hooked the cannula over his ears. A plump Micronesian woman in a brightly printed, homemade skirt clutched an excited toddler; her husband followed, holding a carrier containing an indignant rooster. A businessman in a suit, wearing a white Panama hat, filled a seat near the front.

Stevens rested his head back against the seat, shutting his eyes and wondering when he was going to feel even halfway normal. Everything just took so much effort, and even though his breathing hurt less and he knew his lungs were healing, he was frustrated with looking and feeling injured.

He tuned out the conversation between the pilots as they went through their preflight check, their heads and equipment clearly visible in the open cockpit. Instead he looked at Lei in the seat in front of him.

Her curly head was wedged in between the seat back and the window, propped on a sweatshirt. She looked like she might already be trying to get a nap. The memory of her belly fluttering beneath his hand tried to melt his resolve. Thinking about it reminded him of Kiet and the ever-present regret that he'd never even known his ex-wife was pregnant. He'd missed everything of his son's early existence, and he regretted it. But how would it have complicated his relationship with Lei to have known Anchara was pregnant?

No telling. They might not even have married. He probably would have kept trying to make it work with Anchara for the baby's sake, and the mere thought of that made his stomach knot, reminding him how much it had cost to be with Lei—only to have her cut him off at the knees.

His resolve not to forget or forgive hardened even as one of her errant curls escaped, bouncing over the seat and seeming to reach toward him. He shut his eyes not to see it.

The plane putt-putted down the runway and seemed to heave itself into the sky with a lurch. Stevens looked out his window, down at the familiar airport. Hilo's lush countryside and the khaki-green waters of Hilo Bay spun away below as they climbed. They had to fly the length of the island before they hit the ocean channel that separated the Big Island from Maui, and Stevens enjoyed the play of the clouds and the soaring peak of Mauna Loa, capped with snow, off to the right as they passed the belching caldera of Kilauea below and to the left. The two volcanoes were separated by vast stretches of hardened black lava interrupted by the green mounds of *kipuka*, spots of elevated virgin forest that the lava hadn't covered.

Flying low had its benefits—the island was ruggedly glorious, as savage and primitive as the world might have been in the Jurassic age. He half expected to see dinosaurs feeding on the tree ferns below.

Stevens was pretty sure Lei had fallen asleep, because her head never moved even as the little plane bounced and yawed in the updrafts, causing the rooster to squawk and the child to fuss. He shut his eyes and willed himself to relax. He'd never been a comfortable flier, and the bounciness and the claustrophobia of these little planes were the worst. He'd succeeded in dozing off as they were circling around Haleakala to land on Maui when everything changed.

CHAPTER NINETEEN

STEVENS WAS first aware something was different as the plane, which had been descending toward the airport, rose again with a high-pitched revving of the engine, banking away from its descent through Maui's narrow sugarcane-covered midsection.

Stevens looked out the window at the patchwork of fields. From this vantage point he could see clearly the stages of growth. Fields newly seeded: dark red soil, studded with cane start cuttings in corrugated rows. Then young fields, bright green with new growth. Older fields with fifteen-to-twenty-foot-tall waving grasses, so much like hula skirts. Finally, fields near harvest, gone to tassel and yellowing as they died without water, stalks rich with trapped sugar.

Stevens frowned as they banked away, curving out over Kahului Harbor and bending around the rugged cliffs and narrow road that curved toward Lahaina. Lei still hadn't moved, but he lifted in his seat to see into the cockpit. The businessman in the Panama hat had moved closer to the cockpit, apparently to find out what the problem was, so he waited to hear an announcement.

The Micronesian man began to expostulate to his wife, waving his hands, their language, a flow of rapid liquid syllables, mostly drowned by the roar of the aircraft's straining engine. The toddler cried.

Finally, the announcement Stevens had been waiting for. "Sorry, folks. We've had orders from Kahului Airport not to land. Some sort of emergency. We've been redirected to land at another airport. It's just an additional half hour or so, and we'll put down and sort this situation out."

Stevens frowned. He didn't like the tone, though the words were rational enough. There was an undercurrent of fear in the man's voice that set off his internal cop alarm.

Lei finally lifted her head. "What's going on?" she asked over her seat to him. "I must have dozed off."

"You missed the whole flight, actually. There's some problem at Kahului Airport, so we're being redirected."

"Dammit." She rested her head back in the corner, apparently going back to sleep. He didn't see the point in alarming her with his own suspicions, so he put his head back and shut his eyes as if dozing, but he kept them slightly open.

The businessman, sitting directly behind the cockpit, turned to look back at the passengers. Stevens saw the matte-black gleam of a weapon in the man's hand, his sleeve covering it. The gun was pointed at one of the pilots through the open door.

We are being hijacked.

"What are the chances?" he muttered to himself. This had to be part of the Chang operation. Keeping his eyes cracked, he slid his phone out and thumbed it on. No signal. The hijacker must have a signal blocker; it only made sense. He wondered what story the pilots had had to tell the tower in Kahului, or if anyone had been alerted there.

How had the man smuggled a gun on board? Thinking back on the lax security getting on, he realized how simple it would have been to have a weapon taped by another person under the seat ahead of time, or even sneak one past the pilots, given the simple security at the small-aircraft terminal.

The system counted on it not being worth anyone's time or effort to hijack a tiny commuter plane. Where was there to go out here, with so much ocean and so little land? Whatever happened, he was sure this wasn't just a random hijacker. This had to be connected with their case.

He considered waking up Lei, but the honest-to-God truth was that he was afraid of what she'd do. She was one seat ahead of him, closer to the hijacker, and he wouldn't put it past her to try to take him down. Unarmed and pregnant.

No. He'd think of another solution.

He'd cleaned out his pockets and didn't have anything on him but his phone and the O2 container. The key was going to be how to get closer to the hijacker without tipping him off. Long minutes went by. Stevens breathed deep and slow, filling and resting his lungs, controlling his heart rate as he waited for the right moment to make a move.

The Micronesian family had accepted the change in route, and the dad had taken out some sort of wooden puppet and was making the baby laugh. Lei's head hadn't moved, and the Panama hat of the hijacker was turned toward the pilots.

They flew past Moloka'i without slowing down. Stevens saw the hijacker glance back to see if anyone had noticed and was glad for his pretend slumber as the hat turned back toward the pilots. He'd tried to see the man's face, but it was screened in sunglasses, and all he could make out was that his skin was a color consistent with Hawaiian ancestry.

Stevens mentally calibrated his physical description of the suspect as the plane hummed on and his tension increased. Sweat prickled under his arms as he scanned out the windows, looking for a clue to their destination. Oahu, a rising purplish sea turtle of a shape, rose into visibility off to his right.

Still, they kept going.

Kaua'i, then. It had to be. Kaua'i had a regular airport and a small commuter terminal on the north shore. There was nothing past

Kaua`i and her tiny sister island, Ni`ihau, but the great open ocean and the uninhabitable Northern Hawaiian archipelago. Ni`ihau was unlikely—it didn't even have an airport, was privately owned, and closed to anyone but a small native Hawaiian population who lived there.

He mentally rehearsed his moves. Timing was going to be the biggest factor.

The plane finally began to descend. Up ahead, through the windscreen beyond the pilots, he could see a landmass. It didn't matter what landmass, really. All that mattered was that the pilots had somewhere, potentially, to bring the plane down. They had to be running low on fuel.

He gathered himself and, moving gracefully and quietly, lifted himself out into the aisle. The cannula was still in place in his nose, but the eighteen-inch-steel vessel of oxygen, roughly the diameter of a Louisville Slugger, was concealed behind his body as he moved toward the hijacker.

"Excuse me, gentlemen. I can't help noticing we aren't heading toward Moloka`i, which is closest to Maui," Stevens said, keeping all his attention seemingly on the pilots. He'd snuck up on the hijacker, whose attention was on the pilots and the landmass ahead, and he felt rather than saw the gun lifting toward him.

He swung the oxygen tank up in a vicious arc, hitting the hijacker in the head and knocking the Panama hat off.

The weapon discharged, a boom like a cannon in the enclosed space, and the screams of passengers and crew filled his ears as the plane veered abruptly downward.

Stevens saw a hole, already whistling air, in the bulkhead beside him as he hit the hijacker again, this time on the arm that still held the weapon. The arm broke, the man screamed, and the gun dropped to the plane's inclined floor, sliding away. Stevens whaled the guy another one upside the head, and this time the hijacker slumped out of the seat into the aisle. Stevens dropped the canister.

"Everyone okay up there?" he yelled to the pilots. "I'm a police officer."

"Yeah, we're okay. Correcting our vector," one of the pilots said. "We have to land up here, though. We're losing air pressure."

As if on cue, yellow masks dropped out of the ceiling, dangling and bouncing on their clear plastic tubing. Someone gave a cry of alarm, and Stevens glanced back quickly and saw Lei was out of her seat, comforting the Micronesian woman and helping the family with their masks.

Stevens looked ahead at what the pilots were seeing—a small island, green as an emerald, with forbidding red cliffs. "Is that Kaua`i?"

"Ni`ihau," the pilot responded.

"Can we make it to Kaua`i? If the hijacker wanted you to land there, no telling what's waiting on the ground," Stevens said.

"No. We're losing air, and we don't have enough fuel to circle around to the airport on Kaua`i," the pilot said, his voice sounding tense. "We were only supposed to be going to Maui. This is two hundred and fifty miles past our original destination."

The hijacker had begun to move on the floor, moaning. Stevens bent down and rifled his pockets, but there weren't any other weapons. He pulled the cannula and plastic tubing off his head and detached it from the O2 canister. He hauled the man back upright into his chair, using the plastic tubing to bind the man's arms across his chest, avoiding the broken forearm—and as he did so, he touched something he was pretty sure was a breast.

Frowning, Stevens tweaked off the sunglasses. The man's face was the medium brown of Hawaiian ancestry and his hair was buzzed short, but the contours of the face were suspiciously femi-nine. Lei had come up beside him as he secured the hijacker in the seat. She grasped the chair back as the plane bounced and rocked.

"Nice job, Michael," Lei said. Stevens felt his battered ego swell a bit as his wife lifted the flopping head of the hijacker and took a look at the face. "This is Anela Chang. What the hell?"

"What the hell is right!" Stevens frowned.

"Probably had a plan to take us out down on the island and get away," Lei said. "It can't have been an accident that we're on the same flight together."

"Don't mean to interrupt, but we're going to have a bumpy landing," the pilot yelled. "Get back in your seats and put those oxygen masks on!"

CHAPTER TWENTY

Bᴇɴᴛ ᴏᴠᴇʀ, Lei preceded Stevens back to their seats. She sat and buckled on her seat belt, slipping the dangling yellow oxygen mask over her nose and mouth, glancing over at the Micronesian family's frightened faces and giving them a thumbs-up.

The bullet hole whistled like air being blown across the top of a Coke bottle, and the sound seemed as loud as the straining engines as they approached the forbidding cliffs of Niʻihau way too rapidly. The air pressure was definitely gone as Lei drew in a ragged breath, her ears popping uncomfortably. She felt Stevens's hand on her shoulder. She reached back, her fingers grasping, and he took her hand, squeezing it hard.

The plane bounced in a gust of wind off the cliffs, and the family all shrieked. The pilot turned on the speaker. "We don't have radio contact with anyone down there, and there's no real airstrip, so we're going in hot and radio dead and landing on the road. Just gonna have to roll the dice that there are no other vehicles. Please assume the safety position illustrated on the card on the back of the seat in front of you."

The plane cleared the cliffs, bouncing in updrafts, and Lei could see the landscape ahead: a scrim of trees, open sun-scoured fields, a tiny cluster of houses they whizzed by, and a long, narrow ribbon of road.

Her ears popped again, and she squeezed Stevens's hand harder as they swooped down toward the road. The engine chose that moment to cut out.

Lei leaned her head on her arm against the seat back in front of her, biting her lips to keep from screaming as the plane bounced, deadly silent, descending toward the road. The Micronesian family yelled as they hit the road, and again as they skipped like a stone back into the air, landing again, skipping up again, trees on the right a dangerous blur so close Lei felt like she could touch them.

The plane finally settled all wheels onto the road and rolled eventually to a stop. Lei felt a bubble of hysterical laughter rising.

"I always wanted to see Ni'ihau, the Forbidden Island." She giggled. Everyone knew the remote, seventy-square-mile island was closed to outsiders.

"Well, you got your wish," Stevens said from behind her. He'd already stripped the yellow mask off. "I know everyone wants off this plane, but Anela Chang brought us here for a reason. We need to get our weapons and be ready."

He'd scooped up Anela's Glock somewhere along the way, and now he shot the magazine, checking the cartridges. "Got fourteen rounds here." He rammed it back in. "Can you go check with the pilots on where they stowed our weapons? I'm going to suss out the exit and look for the radio jammer."

"On it." Lei dropped her seat belt and hurried up to the cockpit. "We're worried about follow-up from this hijacker and her crew," Lei told them, with a thumb back at Anela, still slumped in the seat. "Where did you put our weapons?"

The second pilot spoke for the first time. "They're in a locker under the nose. Tell your husband thanks for taking out the hijacker. Crap, that was close." He wore a nametag that read Ben. He swiped sweat off his forehead with a trembling arm.

"Well, you guys did great, too, bringing the plane down safely.

Hopefully, some rescue vehicles will see us and come check us out," Lei said. "In the meantime, we need to locate the radio jammer that's disrupting our cell phones and your communication."

"Absolutely. We'll look." Both the pilots unbuckled themselves. "Can we let the family off the plane?"

All of them looked at the traumatized family. The father was comforting his wife as the toddler wailed non-stop. The rooster added to the cacophony.

Lei looked back at Stevens, crouched by the exit door. "I think we should deplane," Stevens said. "But I'm going out first, getting the weapons. We'll see what happens when I drop the door." He turned the handle and opened the door, stuck his head and shoulders out, looking around. "All clear."

Stevens pushed a lever, and stairs folded out to hit the road. He clambered down and disappeared.

Lei held up a hand to the others. "Just want to see what we're getting into before everyone gets off." She went to the door opening, squatting to take a look outside.

The little Cessna was parked in the middle of the road, and on one side stretched miles of pristine beach, the ocean wave-tossed cobalt and turquoise, palms bent by the breeze marking the edge of the sand. On the other side of the road, an arid, scrubby plain rose to hills scored by the chisel of erosion and anchored by hardy pines. It was stark, barren, and gorgeous. Lei could hear nothing but the wind in the palm trees. She wondered what it would be like to live somewhere this remote.

"Nothing moving out here," Lei said to the pilots. "Any luck finding the jammer?"

"Nothing up in the cockpit," one of the pilots said.

"Maybe the hijacker will tell us when she comes around," the other piped up.

Lei looked over at Anela, and the woman's head was bobbing. She was awake. Lei went back up the aisle and grabbed Anela's short hair and pulled it, hard, lifting her head up against the seat. "Where's the jammer?" she asked.

Anela shook her head and turned her face away.

Stevens called from the doorway, "Looks like it's safe out here, folks. Why don't you all get out, and we'll look around inside for the device that's jamming our phones?"

Lei squeezed out of the way into one of the seats as the pilots brushed between her and Anela and followed the Micronesian family off the plane.

Once they were all off, Stevens came forward and handed Lei the small backpack she used to hold her weapons in their plastic cases. He was still holding the Glock he'd taken from Anela. "Listen, Chang. We know you had something in mind here. What was it? Talk to us."

Anela hawked and spat, and Stevens didn't get out of the way in time. He wiped his cheek, and Lei saw banked fury in his eyes.

"Biggest mistake I made, not killing you both the minute we were in the air," Anela said. "I'm not telling you anything." She closed her mouth, tightening her jaw. A bruise on the side of her face was already purpling, swelling spreading down the side of her head.

Lei had realized something was amiss right after the pilot had announced their change of landing. She'd pretended to be asleep, waiting for the right moment to make some kind of move, not sure what to do or how to do it unarmed. And then Stevens had moved past her, graceful and sneaky, carrying the canister—and the action had happened so fast, she hadn't had time to react or even be afraid for him.

She'd felt a primordial triumph seeing him stand over the crumpled body in the aisle, still holding the oxygen canister. He'd acted quickly and effectively with the means at hand, and while she wanted to bring up their argument and ask how it was fair for him to do a cowboy stunt like that without even warning her, she was too relieved it had worked.

And this was neither the place nor the time for any of those recriminations.

He'd needed to do what he did, and every minute since, Lei saw how stopping the hijacker was restoring his confidence. Maybe he'd forgive her now that he'd had a hand in dealing with their enemy, too.

"Why don't you organize the passengers and we'll all search," Lei said. "I'll guard her."

Stevens nodded and exited down the hallway, and as soon he was out of sight, Lei reached over and squeezed Anela's broken arm. "I got nothing to lose," she hissed at the other woman. "Tell me where the jammer is."

Anela's face had gone so white Lei thought she was going to faint. "Screw you," Anela whispered.

Lei squeezed again, her face close to the other woman's. "You may think you want me and my family dead, but you have no idea how far I'm prepared to go to stop you and your brother. Tell me now and the pain stops. Tell me now, and we'll be good little cops and give you the fair trial you don't deserve."

Anela whimpered as Lei bore down on the broken arm, and finally the woman said, "What does it matter? It's too late for you anyway. It's in the fire extinguisher."

Lei instantly let go of the arm, wondering what Anela meant, and reached up into the bulkhead, where a bright red mini extinguisher was held into a recessed area with a clamp. She unhooked the steel band, and there was the jammer, a small black device the size of a pack of cigarettes, with a short antenna. She dropped it on the ground in the aisle and stomped on it just as Stevens and the pilots reappeared.

"Got the jammer," she said. Anela had shut her eyes. She didn't say anything.

"Well, good thing, because it looks like we've got company," Stevens said. "Got a Jeep coming down the road."

"What do you want to do?" Lei moved away from Anela into the seat behind her and took out her ankle rig from the duffel. She strapped it on.

"I think we should have the civilians hide. If it's locals, they can help us. If they're not friendlies, we can stay in the plane and use Anela as leverage."

"So you think we should run and hide?" The dark-haired pilot named Ben asked. "Not much cover here." The Jeep was fast approaching, red dust purling up in its wake, and the Micronesian family, complete with rooster, had gone over to sit under the scanty shade of one of the palms.

"Let's hope they're friendlies," Stevens said.

The pilots and Stevens got out of the plane, and Lei stayed inside, pointing her weapon at Anela and calling 911.

The connection seemed to take forever to go through. She wondered if they'd even have a signal out here on Ni'ihau—but they must have a tower, or be able to boost the signal from Barking Sands, Kaua'i's nearby military base, because eventually she connected with Kaua'i's 911 operator. Outside the plane, she heard the Jeep pull up and a local, pidgin-accented voice. "You folks need some help?"

Lei let her breath out in a whoosh of relief—the Jeep's drivers were friendly, thank God.

Lei told the operator her badge number and the situation on Ni'ihau. "We need transportation off the island and somewhere to hold the hijacker. Oh, and medical assistance," she explained as she overheard Stevens, the pilots, and the new arrivals talking, their voices animated.

She wrapped up the call after assurances that a police helicopter was on the way.

Coming out of the plane, weapon holstered and guard down, Lei wasn't prepared for a blow to the head. She was unconscious before she hit the ground at the bottom of the steps.

Stevens saw his wife pitch forward off the short flight of steps. He spun away from the man he was talking to, trying to catch her, but he was barely able to break her fall as she landed hard, face down in the dirt. He thought she'd stumbled until he turned her over and saw the slack whiteness of her face and felt a warm ooze of blood on the hand cupping the back of her head.

He lifted her into his arms, his heart hammering. They'd been told she shouldn't take any more blows to the head after her past injuries, and his mouth went dry at the severity of this one.

He turned and looked up into the black bore of a pistol in the hands of one of the pilots. Jim, his name badge read, and he'd been the chattier of the two, a good-looking blond guy in aviator glasses.

The other pilot, Ben, had his hands in the air and shock on his face. "What the hell are you doing, Jim?" the other pilot burst out. "What's going on here?"

"I owe Chang money," Jim told Ben. "Didn't want to get involved, but I had to."

The "friendlies" weren't so friendly after all. The two beefy local guys who'd been the picture of concern a moment ago in their tank shirts and combat fatigues picked up hunting rifles and stepped out of the Jeep. Puffs of red dust rose under their boots as they came to stand on either side of Stevens.

"Go get Anela," one of them said to Jim. "You. Over here," he directed the other pilot. Ben hurried to stand beside Stevens as Jim went back into the plane. Stevens looked over at the palm tree where the Micronesian family had been resting and saw they were gone.

Good for them.

Stevens brushed the curls off of Lei's face, alarmed by her paleness, the freckles like paint flecks on her skin and her black eye's coloration a travesty. He felt the pulse in her neck—it was slow but regular. Her body was slack and unresponsive.

"Got anything for her head?" He held up his bloody hand, the sight making his chest constrict. His voice had gone raspy again, and he felt short of breath. Nothing would be gained by letting stress get the better of him—he had to figure a way out of this situation for both of them.

One of the local guys went back to the Jeep, reached under the dash, and tossed him a beach towel. It was bright yellow with a rainbow and aloha printed on it, and he keenly felt the irony as he wadded the towel under Lei's head to sop up the blood.

Head wounds bled a lot, he told himself. Lei was out, but her pulse was good. She hadn't hit the ground too hard. He'd been in time to deflect some of her fall.

Anela appeared in the doorway of the aircraft, and the dark scowl on her face as she looked at them made him tighten his arms around Lei. "Where are the Micronesians?" she barked.

"Who?" the local guy said. "Didn't see anyone."

"A whole family. They have to be here someplace." Anela gestured at the beach, the open landscape.

"Seems like they got away. We don't have much time now. I heard the woman call for a police helicopter," Jim the traitor said. "Let's go."

"Get in the Jeep," Anela said. "We're out of here."

Anela climbed into the front passenger seat, her injured arm tucked against her chest, and one of the locals got in the driver's seat, setting his rifle beside him. The other Ni'ihau native poked Stevens in the back with his weapon. "Get in. Unless you want us to shoot you right here."

Stevens got to his feet with Lei in his arms. The local guy removed both of Stevens's weapons and Lei's pistol. Stevens's pulse picked up with a beat of hope when the man failed to check either of their pant legs—both he and Lei still had their ankle rigs on.

There was a roll bar and a bench on either side of the open-backed Jeep. Cradling Lei, he waited until Jim and the other pilot had climbed in, sitting to the front, leaving him on one bench near the back and the local guy on the seat across from him, rifle at the ready.

Stevens tucked Lei's head against his shoulder and held her there with the towel padding her head, silently praying she was going to be okay.

He caught the local guy's eye across from him. "We're cops,"

Stevens said. "You do this and they're never going to stop hunting you."

"Shut up!" Anela screamed from the front seat as the Jeep started with a roar. "Shut your mouth or I'll shut it for you, permanently!"

The local guy's face was flat and inscrutable. "Listen to the boss lady," he said. But Stevens thought he saw a flicker of doubt in the man's eyes.

The Jeep lurched forward and tore off up the road. Stevens looked back for any sign of the Micronesian family—there was none. Hopefully, they'd come out when the police helicopter arrived and tell what they'd seen.

The Jeep hooked a sharp right turn off the main road and bounced up a four-wheel-drive track, heading into the mountainous area. Another time, Stevens would have enjoyed the views of rolling, grassy hills slanting upward into cloud cover, the open vista unobscured by any human hand, the ocean a wind-flecked cerulean vastness behind them.

But not today. Today he braced his feet on the channeled floor of the Jeep and pushed his back against the raised side to hold himself and Lei steady on the bench, one hand around the roll bar and the other clasping her close across his lap, trying to keep his wife from being jounced as they crawled through ruts and over rocks. The bleeding from Lei's head had stopped, so Stevens spread the stained towel over her to keep her warm in case of shock.

Why hadn't Anela killed them already? It was obvious she hated them as much as Ray Solomon did. Perhaps the answer was in the two shovels he spotted stowed behind the seats—*if there is no body, there is no crime.* Stevens decided not to worry about that, instead mentally rehearsing different escape scenarios.

He felt Lei wake up, a trembling tension reentering her body. He didn't think the others could tell, and he prayed one last time that she was up to the challenges ahead. He put his mouth down close to her ear and whispered into it.

CHAPTER TWENTY-ONE

STEVENS'S VOICE in her ear was rough. "Pretend you're still out. They're taking us into the hills. Pretty sure we're going to be digging our own graves, so when we stop..." He whispered what he wanted her to do.

She kept herself limp but managed a tiny nod, even with her head pounding like a taiko drum. Her face was turned sideways, one ear against his chest, and she could hear the elevated but steady beat of his heart. She felt the lurching, bouncing movement of the Jeep, heard the growl of its engine as it tackled the slope of the hill. Stevens's body flexed around and beneath her to hold them steady on the bench, his arm pressing her close.

Lei savored a ridiculous but persistent sensation of joy in spite of the pain and danger they were in. She was in her special spot against his heart, where she belonged. Whatever happened next, no one could take that from them.

The Jeep crested a rise and started downhill. Lei kept her eyes closed and body relaxed, but her mind rehearsed what he'd told her to do over and over.

The Jeep stopped. Lei tensed without moving and heard him whisper, "Now!"

Using her abs, she tightened her body hard to sit up even as she reached down with her right hand to the ankle holster, pulling the little six-shot revolver and flicking off the safety as Stevens dumped her onto her feet. She tossed off the towel and spun into a shooting stance. Anela was turning to face her, weapon in hand, when Lei shot her. Lei simultaneously heard the reports of Stevens's gun as he shot the man directly across from them and the traitor pilot sitting beside him.

Anela dropped backward out of sight as Lei turned to shoot the driver in the shoulder as he was turning, reaching for his gun, his mouth open in surprise. He keeled over, falling backward out of the open driver's side door.

Ben, sitting beside Lei and Stevens, raised his hands in the air. His eyes were huge.

Lei grabbed the roll bar as dizziness sagged her knees. She used the bar to hold herself up as she turned her weapon on the guy across from them whom Stevens had shot. He was holding his shoulder, his mouth opening and closing, but he'd dropped the rifle.

Stevens kicked the pilot's pistol and the Ni`ihau man's hunting rifle out of the back of the Jeep. "We have to find something to tie them up with."

As if to punctuate that, the driver had staggered to his feet and was making for the bushes. Lei was in no shape to chase him, so she held her weapon on the two remaining men on the bench. Stevens leaped out the back of the Jeep, running.

He hit the driver from behind, knocking him to the ground. He kept him down with a knee in his back and shouted to Lei, "I need some restraints!"

Lei looked around the Jeep and rifled the men's pockets. She found a pocketknife in the Ni`ihau man's pocket and gave it to Ben.

"Tear up this towel." She handed Ben the bloodstained towel. The young man jumped to help, cutting the tough edging so that he could rip the towel into long strips.

Anela was no longer a threat; nor was she going anywhere. Lei looked away from her body and back at the two she had to keep an eye on.

Things went better after that.

Lei and Ben tied their prisoners, and Stevens secured his. All were moved to lie wedged together in the back of the Jeep, moaning from their injuries but not in danger of dying. Ben and Stevens did some rudimentary first aid as Lei gathered their cell phones and found her own, calling the 911 operator on Kaua`i again.

Once again she identified herself with her badge number.

"Did your team find the downed plane on Ni`ihau?" Lei asked.

"We did. They didn't find anyone there but a family who'd escaped from the hijackers."

"Well, Lieutenant Stevens and I are safe along with Ben, one of the pilots. We have the hijackers and their colleagues in custody, but we have a fatality—Anela Chang, who was hijacking the plane with the help of one of the pilots." Lei looked around at the steep, rocky four-wheel-drive trail and the surrounding wind-scrubbed, brushy area. It looked tough to land a helicopter here. "We can drive to a better location to rendezvous, but we don't want to leave the body— we want to leave it just where it fell for the investigation."

Stevens, crouched by Anela's body, looked at Lei and nodded agreement. Lei finally really looked at the fallen woman.

Anela's pistol was still in her hand. She'd been turning to shoot, but Lei had gotten her first. There was a neat hole in her forehead from the small-caliber round from Lei's snub-nosed ankle piece. She was sure the back of Anela's head was messier. The woman had fallen backward out of the Jeep, and one of her feet, in a business-man's loafer, still rested in the doorframe of the vehicle.

"One moment. Let us triangulate off your phone signal, and then the pilot will set the bird down as close to your location as he can," the 911 operator said.

Lei sat down in the driver's seat and felt the collective extremes of the last few days overwhelm her now that they were safe. Pain was talking to her from all over her body, but most concerning was a clenching in her guts, a punch to the lower back. She puzzled over how she could have hurt herself there, but with falling down the stairs of the plane, there was no telling.

Ben had reclaimed his phone, and they'd allowed him to call his wife—"but no one else until you give your statement." The young man was pacing, talking, and gesticulating. Stevens had picked up one of the hunting rifles and reloaded his holsters. Bristling with weapons, he stood near, keeping an eye on their prisoners and looking out for any intruders.

Lei heard the thrum of the chopper's approach overhead, and she looked up into the deep blue sky. Poufs of dazzling white cloud scudded by, and as she often did, Lei felt the contrast of the beauty around them and the ugliness of their humanity. She leaned her head on the steering wheel, conscious of the dead woman a few feet away, the thumping pain of her head, and of an increasing dull agony in her abdomen.

"You okay?" Stevens asked, frowning.

"I don't think so. I think you better have them take me to the hospital. Something's wrong." Lei wrapped her arms around her waist and raised her eyes to Stevens, feeling her face twist at the pain and her eyes fill with terrified tears. "Something's wrong with Baby."

All the oxygen had gone out of the air. Stevens drew in breaths, but they just burned his lungs. He was smothering: buried, burning, drowning. He flailed, fighting for that last breath.

He woke as his thrashing elbow hit the wooden arm of the chair, sending a jangle of excruciating nerve pain up his arm. He sat up, holding his elbow in the dim glow of the hospital-room floor strip, and glanced over at the bed, hoping he hadn't woken Lei.

She was awake. He saw the gleam of her eyes in the dim light, the shine of tears on her cheeks. He was already as close to her as he could be in the chair, but now he took her hand. "Are you hurting?" he whispered.

They'd given her some sort of medication to stop the contractions she'd been having. She'd been bleeding when they first got to the hospital, but the medicine seemed to have worked because the symptoms had backed off. Lei had refused any pain medications for her head injury, not wanting it to affect the baby.

The hours between when the helicopters had reached them and now were a painful and terrifying blur he hoped never to relive.

"Head hurts," she whispered back. "Tummy hurts. I'm so scared, Michael. I want this baby so much. I never expected to feel this way."

"Me too," he said. He pulled her over so her forehead touched his, and their breath mingled in the warm space between their bodies. "But if something happens, there will be others."

She pulled away from him, crossing her arms over her belly in that protective gesture he was coming to know. "I don't want any others." She turned her face away.

He wasn't going to let her withdraw. He got up and gently moved her over in the bed, climbing in with her, turned on his side so he was wedged beside the support bars. He pulled her into his arms and, when she finally relaxed, her breath smoothing out in sleep, he wriggled them around until he was on his back and she on her side, her head in her special spot, her body stretched along his.

Warm, supported, sheltered.

He could feel their heartbeats falling into the same rhythm.

And when he finally slept, he didn't dream.

CHAPTER TWENTY-TWO

STEVENS SAT WITH THE KAUA'I detectives that had responded to the emergency call from Ni'ihau. He and Lei had been on the medevac helicopter, which had flown her to the closest hospital, Kaua'i's Wilcox Memorial. They'd spent the night there along with the hijackers they'd shot. Stevens had turned both their peashooter revolvers in to the ballistics department, but they'd been too occupied with Lei's crisis to give statements.

"It's been a few years." Lei's former nemesis from her stint on Kaua'i, short, muscular Detective "Fury" Furukawa, clapped Stevens on the shoulder in male camaraderie. "Nice takedown out there."

"Team effort with Lei," Stevens said.

"Yeah. About that," Furukawa said, flipping open a file filled with crime-scene photos of the Jeep. Anela's body sprawled out of the vehicle, one of her feet still caught in the Jeep's door. "How's Lei doing?"

Stevens had the feeling Furukawa was asking strictly for form's sake, and he was glad to know Lei's former partner, Jack Jenkins, and Captain Fernandez, who'd always been supportive, were watching the interview. They had friends, even on Kaua'i, the most remote of the islands.

"Hanging in there. Not in any shape for an interview yet." Stevens pushed a hand through his hair, deliberately turning his thoughts away from Lei, still curled up in that hospital bed.

"Well, then. Why don't you start by walking us through the events."

Stevens gave his statement, grateful when, halfway through, his union rep arrived to sit in. He didn't entirely trust Furukawa or his sidekick, Flea, two men who'd resented his and Lei's presence on Kaua`i when they'd worked there some years ago.

"So, when you whispered to Lei to get up shooting when the Jeep stopped, did you tell her to kill Anela Chang?"

"We were in a life-or-death situation. I told her to 'take out' Anela and the driver, because I thought I could push her up into a better position to shoot them than the men directly across from us, who I was in a better position to get. If I shot at Anela and the driver, I would have had to get Lei off my lap, stand up, turn, aim, et cetera. All we had was speed and the element of surprise. We were lucky it was enough."

"I just find it interesting that Lei shot Anela in the head and the driver in the back of the shoulder."

"We had to use deadly force. Anela has a gun in her hand, as you can plainly see, and Lei was close to her. Too close to miss." Stevens felt his breathing hitching with agitation as he stabbed the photo emphatically with his finger.

"And yet you didn't shoot to kill the men across from you."

"Neither had their weapon at the ready. The Ni`ihau man had set his rifle down on his lap. The pilot had tucked his weapon in his belt. It's a split-second decision. When I fire, I'm prepared to use deadly force in every circumstance—but I took a chance that it wasn't necessary this time. Anela was the only one holding a weapon at the ready."

"And she's one of those behind the attacks on your home and family, if what the Big Island investigators say is true."

Stevens set his jaw and didn't answer. He didn't like where this was going.

"So do you think a head shot was necessary to stop Anela Chang?"

The union rep finally interjected. "Lieutenant Stevens can only speak to his own actions."

"So tell us again how you knew the plane was being hijacked."

Stevens went through it again and again as Fury and Flea tried to find a hole, an inconsistency in the story, a variation that showed Lei and Stevens setting Anela up for slaughter—at least that's what it felt like to Stevens. He was grateful that there were multiple witnesses, especially the pilot Ben, who could corroborate events.

Stevens's phone had been vibrating in his pocket for the last half hour when the union rep finally brought things to a close. Stevens checked his phone. Multiple calls from Wilcox Memorial flashed up at him, and his heart rate spiked.

"Excuse me. I have to see what this is." Stevens stood and turned away to listen to a nurse telling him to return to the hospital. "Your wife's taken a turn for the worse."

Stevens ran out of the interview room, hitting the door with his shoulder. Jack Jenkins, his fresh young face worried, burst out of the observation room to fall into step beside Stevens as he headed for the front doors of the building. "Take me back to the hospital. Lei's having trouble." The lead ball of dread and fear in the pit of Stevens's stomach made him short of breath.

LEI DIDN'T WANT to wake up. There was some very good reason not to, and as the cottony darkness of medication receded, she tried in vain to cling to it.

But slowly, inevitably, as if an unstoppable force like the tide was depositing her on a shore, waves of consciousness pushed her higher and higher into wakefulness. And there was nothing there she wanted.

She remembered now why she didn't want to wake up.

Baby is gone.

Lei's whole body convulsed in a thrashing movement of self-protection as she curled up tight around her empty womb, her arms and legs pulling in close, the IV in her hand snagging on something and bringing her up short.

She opened her eyes. Stevens was there beside her. He reached a fumbling hand to untangle the plastic tubing, trying to keep the needle from ripping out of the back of her hand. She reached up to touch his face.

"Tell me it didn't happen," she begged.

Instant tears filled Stevens's arctic-blue eyes and welled over. Those blue eyes, haggard under dark brows, told her Baby was gone.

"No!" Lei cried. "No! No! No!" She rolled back and forth in the bed, arms tight around herself. The IV needle broke out of her hand, and the rails of the bed rattled as she banged against them.

She knew her wails of grief were inappropriate and weak, and she didn't care. Nothing existed but this terrible rending, this loss of hope, future, and love—the death of someone she'd known in a magical way, if even for a short time, and that she'd wanted to know all her life.

So many losses. All of those losses piled on her. She was drowning in them.

Her childhood, stolen from her by abuse and drugs.

Aunty Rosario, her guardian and beloved *hanai* mom, gone so recently.

Her mother, Maylene, lost to her addiction.

Her grandmother, Yumi, whom she'd never known.

Anchara murdered.

And now Baby.

People came. There were noises and soothing hands and Stevens trying to comfort her, but nothing made any difference, nor ever would. They must have given her something, because finally, merciful darkness closed over her head.

The next time Lei woke up, it was because light was stabbing the backs of her eyes. There was a dull throbbing in her uterus. Her mouth was cottony with thirst, but she also had to pee.

She remembered.

The energy for any movement was gone. She lay still, feeling utterly flat.

Flat and mangled, like roadkill.

Flat as an open desert road with nothing for miles in any direction.

Lei opened her eyes. The room was empty, and she was relieved no one was there. She didn't even want to see Stevens right now. She reached over and pressed the button that lifted the bed up. She noticed her left hand was bandaged where the IV had been torn out. They'd put a new one in her right hand.

Carefully, Lei swung her legs to the side of the bed and used the steel pole with its rolling wheels to help her stand, and shuffling like a crone, she went into the bathroom.

Lei's underwear crinkled with a bloodstained pad as she went to sit on the toilet. Tears welled at the sight. She managed to pee and then got herself back into bed.

The feeling in her body, mind, and heart was like being an Egyptian mummy, she decided. Her organs had been chopped up and pulled out through her aching throat with a hook. Her body was a hollow wreck wrapped in bandages, her soul waiting for some far-from-certain resurrection.

"Ba-ba-ba!" Lei heard from the door, and her eyes flew open.

"Kiet!" she exclaimed. Stevens came toward her holding the baby. Kiet strained toward her, his mouth open with that pearly single tooth gleaming, rooster tail of black hair aquiver.

Lei folded the baby into her arms, and he felt wonderful and smelled perfect, like powder and milk. She burst into noisy tears at how good holding him felt and how utterly devastated she still was. Her emotions were a tornado, swirling and conflicted.

She'd lost Baby, but she still had Kiet.

Kiet went rigid with fright at the sound of her crying, arching his back and letting out an uncertain wail. Lei looked for Stevens to take him, but he and her father were out in the hall, conferring.

This is motherhood, Lei thought. *You get a grip on yourself and do what's right for the kid's sake.* Her own mother had never known how to do that, and Lei wasn't going to make the same mistakes.

Lei gulped down her tears and smiled through them, snuggling and rocking Kiet close. "It's okay, little buddy. Mom's just a little emotional. It's all good." And she blew on his neck gently, and he hunched, even his toes curling up, and made a little sound like a giggle.

Her dad came across the room, sat in the chair next to the bed. "Lei-girl. I'm so sorry."

"Me too." Lei took Kiet's hand, waving it, smiling at the baby to keep tears at bay.

"Wasn't meant to be," Wayne said. "But there will be others."

Lei speared him with a glance. "Please don't ever say that again. Nobody say that again."

Wayne sat back in the chair and ran a hand through his hair. "Sorry, honey. I never know what to say about this kind of thing. Thank God you are both safe. Kiet missed you guys. Fussed all the time. I was at my wit's end when I got the call you were here."

"You did the right thing, bringing him to me," Lei said.

Wayne smiled at her, gratitude in his face. "I didn't know what else to do. He needs his mama."

Stevens came in, carrying a big Starbucks cup and a bag. "Got a chocolate croissant for you."

"Let me start with the coffee," she said. "When am I getting out of here?"

Right on cue, a doctor had appeared in the doorway. He was a grandfatherly, kind-looking Asian man who looked vaguely familiar to Lei. "I'm Dr. Kim. Would you mind taking the baby out for a minute?" he asked Wayne. "I'd like to speak to the parents alone."

"Sure." Wayne got up with alacrity and took Kiet from Lei, carrying him out of the room.

The minute the baby was gone, Lei was aware of her emptiness again. She crossed her arms over her stomach and waited as Stevens sat down on the chair beside her. He handed her the cardboard cup, and she took it for something to do.

"So. You had a spontaneous miscarriage. You were in so much pain and distress, we gave you some pretty powerful medications to assist the process and to keep you comfortable. Then, as you signed consent for, I did a procedure called a D & C to make sure the uterus was clear. You have a healthy reproductive system. No lasting damage that I could determine."

Lei blinked. The tears had started again, and they just kept trickling out. She didn't remember any of it. She'd probably had one of her black-hole memory blips because of the trauma. She took a sip of coffee, her hand trembling. Stevens took the cup from her, taking both of her hands.

Still the tears trickled out of her eyes. "Was it my fault? Did I hurt the baby?"

"No. No, ma'am." The doctor sat down on the edge of the bed beside her and flipped open his folder. "You had some injuries—a slight concussion from a blow to the head, a contusion on your eye. But nothing that would have caused trauma to the uterus or reproductive organs."

"But what about stress causing it to happen? I was really stressed out the last few days. We...we had a house fire. And a raid. And a hijacking."

"No. None of that should have affected the fetus. Tons of stress hormones aren't great for a developing baby, but there have been babies born in the most horrendous of circumstances—in the middle of wars—happy and healthy. Sometimes these things just happen. There's usually something wrong with the fetus." He shut the folder.

His eyes were kind. "Don't blame yourself. Take some time. Enjoy the child you have. And when you're ready, try again. You're young, and there are no problems with your reproductive system that I could see. You should be able to get pregnant again with no trouble."

Lei shut her eyes. She couldn't imagine being ready to take such a risk, but at the same time, the loss felt overwhelming. Never to have a baby, ever...Her brain shut down, unable to deal with the dilemma.

Stevens rubbed her hands. "How soon can we go home?"

"Tomorrow. I want you to stay one more day, just to rule out any complications or blood clots, that sort of thing."

"Thanks, Doctor. I'm sure you did the best you could to help us," Lei said, making herself look at him.

"Thought we'd saved your baby, but it just wasn't meant to be this time," the doctor said, standing up. "Feel better." He left.

Stevens pulled her into his arms. "It wasn't your fault."

"I'll never believe that," Lei said, pressing her face into his shirt, her voice choked. "I should never have gone to the Big Island."

"If we're going to play the blame game, I should have caught you when that asshole pilot cracked you on the head and you fell down the stairs," Stevens said. "I just couldn't get there in time."

"He said that didn't cause it either."

"Well, it couldn't have helped. At least the shroud killer thing's wrapped up. When you feel up to it, Furukawa's waiting to get your statement."

"Oh God." Lei rubbed her tearstained face on his shoulder. "Can I talk to him tomorrow?"

"I think we can fend him off until then."

"Thanks for having Dad come with Kiet. He's just what I need right now."

"I can tell." Stevens rocked her in his arms. "We're going to be okay. We have to be okay."

Lei heard the tears in his voice. They clung together until Wayne came back, and Kiet brought sunshine.

CHAPTER TWENTY-THREE

LEI SAT GINGERLY on the hard plastic seat in the interview room at Kaua'i Police Department. She and Stevens had checked out of the hospital, and Jenkins had given them a ride over to the station so they could leave Wayne with the baby and the rental car at his motel.

Lei looked around at the familiar setting of steel table, chairs, and mirrored observation window. She'd got through the gauntlet of greetings by former teammates at the KPD by sheer force of will, and now the energy it had taken to get here seemed to have leaked out, leaving her drained with the interview with Furukawa still ahead. Their union rep was seated next to her, but Stevens wasn't allowed in the interview. She knew he was in the observation room, and just knowing he was watching strengthened her a little.

Captain Fernandez, dapper in an immaculate uniform, came in, followed by Detective Furukawa.

"Lei! So glad to see you again!" Fernandez extended a hand and shook hers warmly. She'd enjoyed working under him in spite of all the politics of the Kaua'i station, and the smile she gave him was genuine.

"Nice to see you, too, Captain."

"Hope you don't mind. I'm going to be sitting in on this interview."

"Not at all," Lei said, secretly relieved. She'd watched "Fury" Furukawa and his partner tag team interviewees before and hadn't been looking forward to it.

"Welcome back to Kaua`i," Furukawa said. "Wish it were in better circumstances."

"Me too," Lei said, wondering if he was sincere. It was impossible to tell with his blank stare. Those ready tears started to well, and Lei remembered a trick Dr. Wilson had taught her—doing some simple mental math. She ran through a multiplication table and the tears backed off. "Can we get started? I'm still not feeling well."

"Certainly." Furukawa turned on the recording equipment and took a seat beside the captain. He stated the date, time, and persons present for the interview, then started in. "We've collected physical evidence and interviewed all the witnesses at the scene. You're our last witness statement."

"I expected that," Lei said.

"Why don't you tell us what happened, beginning with getting on the plane."

Lei did. It took a while, as Furukawa stopped her for questions or clarification. So far the interview was progressing well, and Lei was relieved. The aggression Stevens had hinted at seemed to have been curbed by the captain's presence.

They came to the part where Lei was taken away by the medevac helicopter. "We heard you lost a baby," Furukawa said. For the first time Lei saw some expression in his eyes, and it was compassion. "So sorry to hear that."

Mental math, mental math. Lei managed to keep the tears in. She nodded. "It's sad, yes."

"Perhaps you'd like to tell us why you were on the Big Island in the first place," Furukawa said.

"I was investigating a gambling operation out of Kahului. Turns out it was a small part of the Chang family crime operation," Lei said. She described the case, emphasizing that she'd been authorized by Omura to go and work with Hilo PD.

"And how did you come to tie that case in with the Chang operation that turned out to have a meth lab in it?"

"I interviewed Terence Chang. He gave me the information. Even showed me where the meth lab was. He's a major witness in that case."

"So you were aware the FBI had specifically directed that you not be involved with any investigation involving the Changs?" Furukawa's face gleamed as he pressed in on her.

"I was aware, yes. But I thought the situation demanded that I follow where the evidence was leading." Lei pinched her leg through the soft fleece pants Stevens had bought her that morning. The pain kept her grounded and alert.

"So the situation of a minor gambling case dictated that you approach Terence Chang for help with your case? Funny, because he says in his statement, 'Lei Texeira approached me at my home to ask who was attacking her family.'"

Lei frowned and stayed silent as the union rep leaned forward and addressed Furukawa. "This line of questioning doesn't have anything to do with KPD and your case on Ni`ihau."

"I disagree," Furukawa said. "I think what happened on Ni`ihau had roots in a homicide twenty-five years ago, involving Lei's father and the head of the Chang crime family. The body count on this feud is getting deep, from what I've discovered. I've contacted Internal Affairs and turned this whole thing over to them."

"Very dramatic," Lei said, even as her gut twisted. She hunched over, breathing shallowly through the pain. They'd told her she might have residual cramping for a while, and the stress wasn't doing anything good for her system.

"Detective Furukawa!" Captain Fernandez exclaimed. He stood, walked to the wall, and turned off the recording equipment. "You're supposed to run all such referrals through me!"

"Begging your pardon, Captain, but if referrals had to go through commanding officers, IA would never have anything to investigate." Furukawa crossed his arms, unrepentant. Lei knew he'd been waiting years for this opportunity to bring her down.

Captain Fernandez turned to Lei. "I'm sorry. I didn't sanction this."

"It's okay," Lei said, standing. "It will be whatever it will be, and frankly, right now I just don't care. I'm not feeling well. You have my statement. I'm going home now." She walked carefully to the door, where Stevens met her. He wrapped a long arm around her and pulled her in against his side.

"Let's go home."

Lei remembered at the same moment Stevens did, by his ironic glance, that they no longer had a home.

CHAPTER TWENTY-FOUR

Hellish WAS the word for their first night back on the property. Stevens and Lei were squished into Wayne's double bed in the one-bedroom cottage, with Kiet in a portable crib beside them. Wayne slept on the couch in the front room.

Kiet slept fine, but Stevens had continued to have nightmares since the fire, and he woke Lei with his flailing. Lei was also having a rough time. She'd cried intermittently all day after they left the police station on Kaua`i, tears rolling quietly down her face, and she moved like a sleepwalker when she moved at all.

Even after Aunty's death, she hadn't been like this. It alarmed Michael to the point that he could hardly grieve the loss of Baby himself, in his worry over his wife's emotional state. The only thing that seemed to perk her up a little was Kiet, so after their first bad night, he handed her the baby and decided to get started cleaning up the mess of their burned house, a stark and ugly reminder of all they'd lost.

With the rubble gone, maybe moving forward would be easier. He'd called Pono and Jared yesterday when they got home from Kaua`i, and they both said they had the day off and would try to round up some friends to help.

They had a budget from the insurance company, but it wasn't much in the scope of having to clean up and replace the house. Still, it was enough to get started, and Stevens needed to work, to throw himself into a project. He got on the phone and ordered a big demolition container and a small Caterpillar bulldozer and driver to come that day.

Stevens pulled on a pair of Wayne's old work pants, surprised to find that, if a little tight in the legs, they fit him. He must have lost weight. He followed those with sturdy rubber boots and gloves and a particle mask.

With his father-in-law at his side and a shovel and ax in his hand, Stevens waded into the pile of dangerous burned material that was all that remained of their house.

They worked for a couple of hours. The sweat of effort felt good, stinging Stevens's eyes and loosening his muscles. He hauled burned wood into a pile, chopping down larger pieces, Wayne right alongside him with a wheelbarrow. He straightened up, ax in hand, as several trucks pulled up their driveway.

Pono's purple truck was in the lead, the bed filled with buff young men in work clothes. Jared's truck followed, and Stevens recognized firefighter friends he'd been introduced to following in their vehicles. Bringing up the rear of the vehicles lumbered a tractor-trailer with the Cat and a giant dumpster.

Stevens felt his chest swell with suppressed emotion as the vehicles unloaded. Men carrying tools and wearing protection gear climbed out, laughing and talking. Jared had made sure they were dressed properly for dealing with fire debris.

His brother approached, blue eyes alight with energy and determination. "Brought a bunch of off-duty friends."

Stevens embraced Jared, clapping him on the back hard with a blackened glove. "Got the first charcoal of the day on you, bro. I can't thank you enough."

Pono approached, wearing a pair of rubber waders. He thumbed back at the cluster of men climbing out of his truck.

"Rounded up these lame-asses to help. Point 'em at it and they'll go all day."

"Thanks, man," Stevens said. "What's up with the waders?"

"Tiare suggested these." Pono shrugged. "She had some idea I'd be able to rescue my clothes."

"Good luck with that." Stevens pulled off his gloves and did introductions and shook hands with the men, moved by the enthusiasm on their faces to wade into the giant pile of debris. He coordinated with the Cat driver and they positioned the dumpster, and soon the property was humming with the efforts of a mobilized community of police officers and firemen.

Stevens felt good, even though the sweat dug runnels through the black on his face. He set the pace with his shovel.

Lei sat on the tiny porch of the cottage, bouncing Kiet on her knees as she watched the beehive of activity in her yard. Tears rolled down her cheeks, but she made no sound.

They had friends who cared about them, pitching in to help in their time of need. She could hardly believe the number of men and the pileup of vehicles cluttering the yard. It was good to see Stevens right in the midst of it, swinging tools and directing the cleanup.

But even with all this activity, she just didn't feel anything but flat. Even in her grief for Aunty Rosario, she'd known what she was feeling. This numbness was different.

She put her nose into Kiet's neck and breathed. He kicked his legs at the touch of her mouth on his neck, and she smiled.

"Lei." Pono had come up on her steps, wearing a ridiculous pair of rubber waders and his ever-present Oakleys. "I heard. So sorry, Sweets."

"Yeah." Lei rubbed her cheek on Kiet's head. "Thank God I have this little guy to keep me busy."

"Heard about that IA bullshit, too. Can't wait to give my statement about the shroud killer and what you've been putting up with this last year."

Lei shrugged. "It will be what it will be."

Pono frowned. "That doesn't sound like you. You gotta come out fighting."

"I'm sick of fighting."

Pono shook his head. "You're grieving. I get it. We lost one in the middle, between our two kids. Never thought we'd get over it, but life goes on. You'll be okay." He turned away, clapping on a hard hat someone had handed him, and stomped back into the black debris.

Lei stared after Pono, her oldest friend and most trusted partner. His rough wisdom, even couched in his own experience, did nothing for her. Maybe the IA investigation would find her guilty of murdering Anela Chang, of orchestrating some elaborate setup, or at the least, of participating in a feud worthy of the Hatfields and McCoys. She just couldn't bring herself to care right now, and there was nothing to be done about it anyway.

It will be what it will be.

Kiet wriggled and fussed, and she carried him into the cottage and fixed a bottle. She was just sitting down with him on the little couch when the front door opened.

Her best friend, Marcella, stood there, big chocolate-brown eyes shiny with tears, hands on curvy hips and lush brunette hair wind-blown. "Lei!" she exclaimed. "Why didn't you call me?"

Lei's ever-present tears spilled. "I couldn't. I just couldn't."

Marcella rushed over and sat beside Lei, hugging her. Kiet watched, bottle in his mouth, secure in Lei's arms.

Sophie Ang, more reserved, arrived in the doorway.

"Stevens called us," Sophie said. She was arresting in a black tank and yoga pants, cropped head high and skin like burnished bronze over toned muscles. "I was so worried about you after that weird call from the Big Island. Marcella flew back from California, and we came over together."

Lei hadn't thought she could cry harder, but at the thought of her husband calling her friends, bringing them here to support her, she buried her face in Marcella's shoulder and sobbed.

Sophie swooped in and plucked Kiet from Lei's arms, rocking

him as she held the bottle and cooed at him. Lei would have been surprised at Sophie's ease with him if she hadn't been crying so hard.

Stevens appeared in the doorway, as filthy as Lei had ever seen him, face black with soot and smeared with sweat. He grinned, and his teeth were startlingly white. "Thanks for coming," he said. "So glad you both could make it."

"Yeah, I'm nothing but a constant waterworks," Lei said, reaching for a tissue. "Sick of it already, but I don't know how to turn it off."

"It's okay. You guys have been through a lot," Marcella said, her arms still around her friend. "Take the time to rest and recover."

"Someone has to take care of Kiet, so it's working out okay," Lei said. "There's just so much to do."

"I'm going to help," Sophie said. "Soon as I decide what outfit to ruin. Might as well be what I've got on."

"You gotta have boots and gloves, at a minimum," Stevens replied. "Lots of rusty nails and such in there."

"I've got plenty of extra gear." Jared had come up on the porch behind Stevens. "Good to see you lovely ladies again. I remember meeting you at the wedding."

"Yes, I remember meeting you." Sophie slanted him a glance and inclined her head, preoccupied with the baby.

"Lei's told us a lot about you. All of it complimentary, by the way," Marcella said. "Thank God you were there to help."

"He's the reason we got out of the house alive," Stevens said.

"It's what I do." Jared smiled, a bright flash in his soot-streaked face. "Great to see you two again. Either of you single? Or both, perhaps? That would be my lucky day."

"All right, bro, rein it in," Stevens said, mock punching his brother's shoulder. "The girls just got here. Maybe we can all go out tonight if Lei is feeling up to it."

Lei forced a smile. "Let's wait and see."

"Well, I'm ready to get dirty if you've got some gear for me,"

Sophie said, and handed Kiet to Marcella. "Show me where to suit up."

"It would be a shame to cover any of you up, but I guess we have to at least protect the extremities," Jared said. "Follow me."

Stevens waved goodbye and followed Jared and Sophie down the steps and back into the rapidly shrinking debris.

Marcella looked down at Kiet. "Too bad I'm taken. Your uncle is a firefighter fantasy come true."

"Yeah, and he's a good guy, too," Lei said. "Bit of a player. I think Sophie could take him, though."

"Sophie can take anyone she wants; she's just picky as hell," Marcella said. "Speaking of, I'm not just taken. I'm officially taken." She extracted her left hand from under the baby and extended it for Lei to see a sparkling engagement ring.

"Oh, Marcella! Gorgeous!" Lei admired the channel-set diamond. "So glad you decided to go for it. Doesn't get any more perfect than you and Marcus."

"Yeah, it does. You and Stevens." Marcella looked at Lei. "You guys are so beautiful together. Building a family despite everything."

Lei brought her hand up to cover her mouth, her eyes filling as she looked at her friend. "You have no idea how hard it's been lately. It's like we made it through the wedding, and then a shitstorm broke. It's been non-stop ever since. I don't know if we're going to make it."

"You'll get through it. You've been through so much already. I don't know if I'd have the courage to take a chance on Marcus if I didn't see it working with you guys. Some risks are worth taking."

Some risks are worth taking.

"Maybe you're right. Since you're diving in, why don't I show you how to change a diaper?" As Marcella laughed, Lei suddenly knew Marcella was right—and so was Pono. Some risks *were* worth taking, and she *was* going to be okay.

Maybe not today, or tomorrow, or in a month, but she was going to be okay.

CHAPTER TWENTY-FIVE

"SOME COPS WANT to talk to you," the correctional officer said, inter-rupting the Fireman's hand of cards with Pork Chop, a tatted-up meth dealer who wouldn't take no for an answer on playing. The Fireman folded his hand and stood up, relieved. He already owed Pork Chop more than he ever expected to be able to pay back.

"See you when you get back," Pork Chop said, with that look he had, as if you'd taste good and he might take a bite.

The Fireman hunched his shoulders, wishing he'd died when he tried to kill himself in the hospital. Instead, he'd woken up to a white light—not the white light of heaven, but the brilliant lamps of a surgery unit.

He'd lived, recovered, and gone to jail to await his trial, unable to make the high bail that had been set due to indications of flight risk. The month he'd been in Maui County Correctional Center felt like an eternity.

He followed the officer down the hall and out through a couple of sally ports to the open visiting area. MCCC wasn't high security, so he wasn't handcuffed as he followed the guard to sit at a small, round table. Other inmates were visiting families in the group setting, but so far, these two cops were his only visitors since he'd been in.

It reminded him again how alone he was.

He sat down and raised his eyes to the woman cop—and stood back up again, terrified.

It was the woman from the house he'd burned. She was even prettier in person than on the video, with curly hair, a slender build, and big, sad brown eyes.

"Please sit down and talk with us," she said.

"We just want some information." The tall man had crystal-blue eyes that contrasted with dark brown hair and a ruggedly handsome face. The grainy black and white surveillance video hadn't done either of them justice. "We know you've already been interviewed several times. We just have a few more questions for you."

The Fireman sat down cautiously. "They've charged me with attempted murder of a police officer, among other things. I swear, I didn't know you were cops."

"Let's back up a minute and introduce ourselves. I'm Lieutenant Michael Stevens. This is Sergeant Leilani Texeira. We're not talking to you as part of the investigation, and we don't mean you any harm."

"You should mean me harm," the Fireman said. "I burned your house."

"Did a good job of it, too," Stevens said. "Our dog and I barely got out alive."

"I didn't mean for it to be such a close shave. I left the kitchen door open so you could get out. I'm an arsonist—I admit it—but I'm no murderer."

"Got a John Doe body in the morgue that disagrees with that," Stevens said. His steady, piercing gaze felt like a laser to the Fireman.

"That was an accident."

"Things happen that you don't mean when playing with something as dangerous as fire," Texeira said. "So you're not a murderer, but you set a really deadly fire in our house, and from what we can tell of your MO, it was the first time you ever burned a house."

"Yeah. I was being blackmailed." The Fireman struggled for a moment with his conscience, then said, "I was paid, too. Paid and blackmailed."

"So someone found out you were doing the cane fires and paid you to burn the house?"

"Yes. And made it clear that if I didn't, they were going to turn me in. They offered me a five-thousand-dollar bonus for any fatalities. I told this to the other cops who interviewed me. I decided to try to get the money but not kill anyone. Keep the blackmailer off my back. But...after the fire, he contacted me again. Wanted me to find a way to burn you in the cottage." The Fireman looked down at his hands. "I'd found out you were cops on the news. Knew I was in deep and it was only going to get deeper. So I tried to run."

"And then I came to the door, and you had a heart attack," Stevens said.

"Yeah."

A pause.

"Can you tell us anything about the blackmailer?"

"He had a lot of surveillance video on you and your family."

The cops looked at each other. The Fireman could tell they hadn't known this. "What else?" Stevens asked.

"He had plenty of money. Contacted me on a phone with texts, delivered stuff he wanted me to use, like the tranq gun, via UPS. He was watching me. I thought it was through the window at first, but now I think he had my apartment wired, too. So he knows technology."

"That's how they're going to prove the case against you in court," Stevens said. "Your online footprint on the forums. On your computer."

The Fireman shrugged. "It doesn't matter. I'm in here, where I deserve to be."

"I want to thank you for not trapping my husband and family in the house," Texeira said. "You could have. So easily."

The Fireman gazed into her sad eyes and felt his own fill.

"I'm sorry," he said. "And I'm sorry about that man that died in the cane field. Sorry for all of it."

Stevens and the woman stood up. "Thanks. That helps," Stevens said. Texeira nodded, and they both shook his hand before they left.

Stevens slung an arm around Lei as they exited Maui County Correctional and walked to his Bronco. "Interesting. We were seriously surveilled by someone familiar with technology. That still points back to Terence Chang."

"I don't think it's him. Really. I think it was Anela and Ray." Lei paused at the vehicle as he beeped it open.

"Well, I'm glad we went and talked to him. The team that replaced me on the case hasn't kept me up to speed at all." Stevens got in on his side and Lei on hers. He slammed the door and fired up the truck. "It's going to be interesting to go to Ray's trial."

"You know the shroud killer thing isn't coming up at all during that," Lei said. "Other than the one shroud in the back of his truck, there's nothing tying him to us at all. He said Anela was the one."

Stevens was glad they were finally having a chance to talk the situation over. In the month following Lei's miscarriage, the days had been filled with cleaning the property, haggling with the insurance company, and periodic interviews with IA and the investigators on the various cases. Stevens had returned to his station, as had Lei after two weeks of medical leave.

"Why do you think Anela was taking us into the Ni`ihau hills?" Stevens asked her. They'd been asked this by Furukawa and others but hadn't compared answers.

"I think she was just as involved with the shroud thing as Ray. His testimony at first was just trying to deflect, to get attention off her. He was hoping she'd escape.

"So then she found out from someone what flight we were on and took the initiative to have us land on Ni`ihau, where she had connections. Those men owed the Changs gambling debts, according to their statements."

"If you hadn't knocked her out with that oxygen tank, I'm pretty sure she'd have rendezvoused with her honchos and disappeared from us permanently. Probably would have taken the plane alone somewhere and disappeared from there."

"Exactly what I thought. Good thing we had so many witnesses on how it all went down." Stevens rubbed the tiny heart tattoo of lei on his inner arm. "The defense is going to try to paint us as the aggressors."

Lei slanted a glance at him, a sparkle in her eyes he hadn't seen in a month. "I think you were pretty aggressive with that canister. Makes me a little weak in the knees thinking about it."

"Oh yeah?" The blood seemed to rush from his head down to a neglected part of him that missed his wife very much. He'd left her alone after the miscarriage, just holding her at night through one or the other of their nightmares. Dr. Wilson had come and done trauma debriefing with them, but there was no quick fix for their losses and grief.

He'd resolved to be patient and wait until she was ready to be with him again. *However long it takes.* She'd never know how hard it was to keep his hands off her night after night.

"Yeah. You were my hero that day." She smiled, slow and sweet.

"You know what, Lei? I've thought long and hard about what you did on the Big Island and how you did it. And while I'll always wish you'd told me and we'd tackled it together, you were right to take initiative. The Changs were just going to keep coming after us until we were dead. Thinking of Anchara, how vulnerable she was pregnant—I couldn't have handled it if it had been you and our child." Stevens cleared his throat. It had been hard to find the right time to say these words, but he'd needed to for a while.

She twined her fingers with his. "I've been hoping you'd forgive me for the Chang thing. But I can't forgive myself for losing Baby."

"It wasn't anyone's fault. Like the doctor said, sometimes these things just happen. Now, we have a house to build. And I for one am glad we're going with cement block this time around."

THE NEXT DAY Lei put the finishing touches on the tent she'd set up a good long way across their yard from the cottage, tucking it behind one of the mango trees out of view. She'd bought the tent on the sly, blown up an air mattress, and purchased beautiful new linens she'd washed ahead of time. She'd put a silky carpet down and hung tiny, golden, battery-operated Christmas lights inside, creating a cozy, romantic getaway—which was what she felt like they needed to be intimate again, with the close quarters they kept with Wayne and Kiet.

A dozen times in the last week she'd almost reached for Stevens, feeling a growing hunger for him—but she'd held back, feeling constraint. Kiet woke easily, and Wayne being right on the other side of their thin wall didn't help an increasing worry that they'd lost their connection, their passion. That inhibition kept her on her side of the bed.

Stevens, other than tenderly holding her when she cried, or letting her hug him during a nightmare, kept his back turned and gave no sign he wanted anything more.

She looked out the entrance of the tent toward the new foundation and the beehive of workmen putting up the cement-block construction in record time. Half the men out there were off-duty friends, refusing to accept payment for their work. They couldn't have rebuilt the house otherwise, as the insurance money had barely covered contractor and material costs.

Lei savored the feeling of gratitude she'd been able to feel again, as the intense grief of losing Baby receded and her body recovered. They had much to be grateful for, even if uncertainties like the IA investigation remained.

Wayne and Kiet had gone to spend the evening at a friend's, so she took a shower and dressed in a silky black robe with nothing on underneath. She was preparing a simple dinner when Stevens drove up. He walked up the steps, running a hand through his hair, and those blue eyes widened at the sight of her. He gazed at her short, silky robe, and her cheeks heated.

"Where's Wayne?"

"Out for the evening. It's just us. Why don't you shower? Dinner will be ready by the time you're out." Lei sipped from a glass of Chardonnay and eyed him flirtatiously over the rim.

"Don't mind if I do." He moved with alacrity into the bathroom, and she smiled, setting the table. She'd made her favorite old standby, teriyaki chicken and rice, and she was seated when he came out, wearing a soft old pair of jeans, nothing else, and toweling his hair.

Lei admired the contours of his chest. Work on the house had hardened and chiseled him further, and it showed in the spread of his shoulders, the narrow V of his abs disappearing into the jeans.

She felt a tingle, looking at him. She'd decided it was time, but she hadn't felt a tingle like that since *before.*

Things were divided into 'before' Baby and 'after.' She wondered if they always would be. She poured him wine, and he sat down and raised his glass.

"I was thinking about our conversation the other day. You said I was your hero. Well, Lei, you're *my* hero." Stevens extended his glass to clink with hers. "To heroes."

They drank.

Lei felt time slowing down. Each moment intensified, all her senses sharpening as she let herself become attuned to him again. The wine was both cool and heating in her mouth, and she felt the movement of her throat to swallow. Light shone on the sprinkling of hair on his chest, gilded the length of his fingers. She smelled the scent of him, soap and man and uniquely hers. Those blue eyes she loved intensified as he gazed at her, unblinking, from under dark brows.

Her hand trembled as she tried to cut her chicken. "I'm scared," she whispered.

"My Lei? Scared?" He took her utensils out of her hands and set them down. Held her cold hands in his warm ones. "Of me?"

"No. Of...loving again. I feel like I've forgotten how."

He took her hand, drew her up against him as he stood. "I've heard it's kind of like riding a bike."

They abandoned the dinner, and she kept hold of his hand and led him out the front door, down the steps through velvety-warm darkness, across the lawn, and around the scarred area where their new house rose, and to the mango tree.

The lights were aglow inside the tent.

"This is...perfect," he said. The tent, lit from within like it was garlanded with fireflies, was a jewel-like setting for the inviting bed. Stevens unzipped the door and held the screen aside for her.

Lei passed close as she entered. She saw the hairs on his arm rise as she brushed him. She felt her nipples tighten in response. The electricity between them seemed to crackle in the air. Still, Lei felt shy, uncertain, fumbling with her hands, pushing them into her pockets, and clumsy in her body.

She sat down on the air mattress and turned toward him, her arms around her knees. He knelt in front of her. "Relax. There's no hurry. There's no one here but us. We can take all the time we want. We don't have to do anything but kiss if you don't want to."

"I know. I've gotten so used to having Kiet close, it feels strange being without him," Lei whispered. "I just feel shy." She reached out and traced his face, her hand sliding down his cheek over the slight stubble there, along the hard line of his jaw. Her fingers brushed his lips, and they felt warm and supple.

He caught her hand in his and kissed her fingertips, drawing the pads of her fingers into his mouth. His tongue darted out to touch them, igniting tiny shocks of sensation that rippled through her body.

Lei felt her breath speed up, and she wanted to be closer to him. She opened her knees and slid forward so that her thighs clasped the rough fabric of his jeans as her silk-clad body pressed against his shirtless chest.

Their mouths touched, fused. Passion rose as they kissed. Their hands wandered and stroked. Touched. Traced and explored.

Smoothed and discovered.

Reknowing.

Rediscovering.

Rekindling.

He groaned. "I know I told you there's no hurry...but it's been so long. I might embarrass myself."

"That's okay," she whispered. "I want you. I need you."

Her arms circled him and drew him down and in, and it was breathless pleasure and the deepest love, the kind only those who've been burned can know.

Turn the page for a sneak peek of book nine of the Paradise Crime Mysteries, *Rip Tides!*

SNEAK PEEK

FIRE BEACH, PARADISE CRIME MYSTERIES BOOK 8

Ocean the color of gemstones—turquoise and lapis, with a few emer-
alds thrown in—seemed to mock Detective Lei Texeira with its
beauty as she pushed through the ring of spectators on the beach at
Ho'okipa, Maui. A couple of uniformed officers she was familiar
with were holding back the crowd, and Lei gave them a nod. "Push
them back further. Put up some scene tape."

Before she looked at the body she'd come for, Lei's eyes swept
the crowd. The onlookers were subdued—all but one, a brunette
young woman in a towel. She was sobbing into the arms of a friend.
Lei made a mental note to come back to her. She turned to her partner, Pono Kaihale.

"Can you start getting names and contact info before these
witnesses start drifting off?"

God bless Pono. Her long-time friend never had a problem with
her taking the lead. He nodded, whipped a notepad out of his pocket
and waded back into the crowd as Lei turned to face the famous
victim.

Kea Simmons lay on his back in the golden, large-grained coral
sand of the beach, deep gouge marks showing where he'd been
dragged up from the foamy aqua waterline. Doing a quick visual, Lei

couldn't see any sign of injury. The young man's eyes were shut, always a mercy. His wet hair, strands of blond and brown, tangled to muscled shoulders. His body was magnificent, wide shoulders tapering to a narrow waist, and sun-bronzed as a surf god.

Which he was.

Even Lei, who didn't follow surfing closely, knew Kea Simmons was Maui's rising surf star and had been looking good to take the prestigious Triple Crown of Surfing this year, with two of the three Oahu events in the contest already won.

Now he lay on the sand in front of her, dead as a piece of driftwood.

Lei felt a clench in the area of her heart. She'd never gotten used to the waste of a young person's death, and she hoped she never did. Staring down at the handsome face reminded her again of how much she herself had lost in this past year—and it was too much to think about now. The familiar yawning hole of grief sucked at her.

One of the paramedics stood up from where he was organizing his lifesaving equipment and Lei turned to him. "What can you tell me?"

"Got the call from the lifeguard tower." The paramedic pointed to the bright yellow, two-story metal structure at the end of the beach. "Said they had a drowning. Didn't know it was Kea Simmons until I got here. Lifeguards brought him in from the surf lineup."

Two lifeguards were standing, hands on hips, their heads close together as they talked, their faces somber. Lei caught the eye of the taller of the two, a muscular Hawaiian wearing red lifeguard shorts. She gestured for him to come talk. He and his partner, younger and slighter, came across the beach.

When Lei had their attention she said, "I'm going to need to interview each of you. I've called the medical examiner, Dr. Gregory, and he should be here any minute to examine the body."

The Hawaiian lifeguard nodded. He extended his hand to shake hers. "I'm Sam Koele. I saw the surfers waving for help in the lineup and went out. Two of them were holding Kea up. Soon as I signaled my partner, he joined me in the water and we got him in to the beach as fast as we could. Started CPR, but he was never responsive."

Dr. Gregory the ME pushed through the crowd, which had swelled as the news of the surf star's death spread via "coconut wireless" gossip. Pono had his hands full trying to nail down witnesses, Lei saw, as the crowd ebbed and flowed.

"Just a minute." Lei pulled her radio off her belt and called for reinforcements to help their team grab anyone who might be a viable witness. The portly ME, whom she knew from various cases, was wearing one of his trademark aloha shirts. This one was decorated with surfing Santas for December. He waved to Lei with a gloved hand as he signed in with the patrol officer on the log.

"These are the paramedics who tried to revive the victim for you to talk to," Lei told the doctor as he approached. Dr. Gregory, usually talkative and good-humored, had sobered at the size of the crowd and the celebrity of the victim. He nodded and with his assistant, Tanaka, knelt in the sand beside the body to begin their assessment.

"Can you help me identify the rescuers who were helping Kea in the lineup?" Lei asked, turning back to Sam Koele.

"Sure. I thought you'd need to take statements once we saw Kea wasn't reviving, so I asked them to wait on the steps." He gestured to where two surfers sat on the metal stairs of the lifeguard tower. Lei had missed them with the lifeguards standing in front.

"Thanks. I'll talk with them next. Did you know the victim?"

"I did. Great kid." The lifeguard blinked his eyes hard and Lei could see moisture in them. "Always friendly and down-to-earth. He's been surfing here for years."

"Tell me what you saw when you first approached him in the water."

"Well, I was using ol' Kelly here." Sam pointed to a huge white surfboard with a red cross on it. "This is our rescue board. We use it as our primary rescue device at this beach with all the surf we deal with here."

"Kelly?"

"After Kelly Slater. Best all-around surfer in the world." Sam's teeth flashed in a brief smile as they both looked at the cumbersome board propped against the metal stairs of the tower.

Lei set her hands on her hips as she swiveled to take in the whole scene. Ho'okipa Beach Park was a crescent moon of beach tucked inside rugged, black-boulder-strewn bluffs. Fifty to a hundred yards from shore, she could see three different areas where surfers clustered in the water around breaking waves.

She and Stevens had been beginner surfers for some time now, so she knew the riders were gathered around wave peaks that broke regularly in a certain spot, a predictable point where surfers could "line up" with a geographic marker of some kind on the beach and be positioned to take off. A good deal of the skill of surfing was being in the right place at the right time to get an optimal position on a wave, and that was rarely accidental.

"Which peak was he at?"

Sam pointed. "Over there."

Lei looked. He'd been at the Point, the first of the peaky areas. Today the surf was pretty big, coming in at around six feet in wave face height from trough to crest of the wave. Even as Lei looked, a surfer took off, making the drop and pulling up to position himself for a tube ride, where water covered him and he was able to travel inside the wave—and then Lei saw another rider drop in on him, spoiling the ride by blocking his passage.

The wave closed over the first rider and Lei saw him disappear, wiping out. She frowned, watching the surfer who'd stolen the ride, on a green board, pump his way down the wave as it broke and finally kick out at the end.

"Did you see that?" Lei asked Sam. Getting caught inside a barrel, hitting another surfer's board or the bottom, even tangling with one's own board in a wipeout were all common hazards that could cause death—but it would be highly unusual for a surfer of Kea's ability to drown in such relatively minor water conditions.

"Yeah. There's been a lot of bad manners in the water lately,"

Sam said. "I've had to break up quite a few beefs on the beach." Even as they watched, the first surfer who'd lost the wave was yelling, pumping his board through the water toward the surfer who'd stuffed him in the barrel. He smacked the water and cursed when he reached the other surfer. The drop-in surfer shrugged and moved off.

"So tell me what you saw when you got to Kea and his rescuers," Lei went on.

"They were holding him on the front of one of their boards. Both of them had rescued him and said they'd found him face down, floating. They said they saw Kea take off on a wave and they were watching him because they were paddling back out. Then another surfer dropped in on him, and both of them wiped out. Or at least, that's what it looked like to them. But the other surfer paddled away, and Kea's board came back up without him."

"Where's that other surfer?" Lei focused on Sam's face. She saw something in his weathered brown features—a tightening of the lips, a narrowing of eyes bracketed by fans of wrinkles from squinting into the dazzle of sea and sun.

"They said they didn't know. He paddled back out, and by the time they got Kea up and out of the impact zone where the waves were breaking, they couldn't see him anymore."

"So he's not that guy that just snaked somebody again?" Lei asked. The aggressive surfer they'd been watching had just dropped in on another rider.

"No, but dat buggah goin' get in scraps when he come in," Sam said, lapsing into pidgin, frowning. "Okay if I call him out of the water?"

"Yeah. That's dangerous, what he's doing. I want to see if he's the guy Kea tangled with."

Sam jogged to the lifeguard tower, said something to the surfers, retrieved a bullhorn and an air horn, and climbed the steps of the tower. He blew the air horn and everyone on the beach jumped.

"Surfer on the green board, exit the water," he bellowed into the megaphone. Lei started at the loudness of the bullhorn. She turned to look out at the man who'd been violating surfing etiquette and was surprised to see that, instead of exiting the water as he'd been ordered, the man was paddling downwind toward the next break as fast as his arms would propel him.

Sam repeated his direction.

"Stupid," Lei said to Pono, who'd materialized at her side. "Where the hell does he think he's going?"

"Out to sea, looks like."

Sam returned, his dark eyes flashing with irritation. "Want me to catch him on the Jet Ski?"

"Yeah. Bring the fool in," she said. "Where does he think he can get away on a surf board?"

Lei walked toward the lifeguard tower and the two men who had rescued the victim as Sam and his partner ran back and drove a quad with a Jet Ski already trailered on the back, across the beach. Sam's partner turned the quad and backed the vehicle down into the shifting sand, lapped by surf as Sam guided the 'ski off the trailer and into the water.

Sam then jumped aboard, flipping down a floating rubber tow mat, and throttled the engine, turning the craft to zoom across the choppy inside of the bay toward the fleeing surfer. The surfer had made it all the way past the last Ho`okipa break.

Backup patrol officers had arrived, and Pono was organizing them to canvass the crowd. Dr. Tanaka and Dr. Gregory had erected a privacy shield, a pop-up metallic-looking tent, over the body to screen out the sun and prying eyes as they did undignified things to what remained of Kea Simmons.

Lei refocused her attention on the two rescuers. "Tell me what happened," she said.

Lieutenant Michael Stevens sometimes wished he wasn't so good at his job. If he weren't, he wouldn't have been given new duties. Stevens rubbed a knot of tightness between his brows. He'd got the unwelcome news that, due to budget cuts, his little station out in

Haiku was being reabsorbed into bigger Kahului Station. He was keeping his rank, but he'd been reassigned by Captain C.J. Omura to be the head-training officer for new detectives.

Stevens sighed as he set his station's expenditure report down. Glancing out the door of his office, he could already see his men packing up—at least he wouldn't have to work on budget reports anymore, and he got a raise. But he didn't like the idea of not having his own active cases.

He took one of a stack of cardboard boxes he'd picked up behind Foodland and began cleaning out his desk.

"Boss." Detective Joshua Ferreira, closest thing he had to a partner, knocked on the doorframe. "Want I should get some guys to bring their trucks to move all this furniture?"

"I have to check with the captain, see how much of it is already down at Kahului and how much we're going to have moved into the state storage facility," Stevens said. "Thanks for reminding me." He picked up the phone and rang through to Omura's office.

"Yes." Omura always sounded clipped and in a hurry. It kept calls short and made her more efficient, he realized, but he never looked forward to calling her.

"Hey, Captain. What do we do with the furniture here? Are you putting all the men in with other details, or will we have our own corner in the building?"

"In with the rest. You can tell them their reassignments," Omura said. She rattled off the six men's names and their new assignments. "Just take your personal things out of the building. We'll have to squeeze you guys into the existing space, and we'll have the Building Division move the Haiku furniture into the big storage facility."

"Okay," Stevens said. "What about where you're putting me?"

"You're going to share an office with the recruiter and new officer trainer, Eric Tadeo. I told him you're coming."

"Great," Stevens muttered.

"Excuse me?"

"I said, great. Whatever works for the department," Stevens said louder, with false cheer.

"Good." Omura hung up with a click.

He sighed again and stood up. Ferreira was still waiting in the doorway. "We're all being reassigned and the stuff goes into storage," Stevens said. "I have everyone's assignments. Tell the guys to come in."

He continued to gather up and sort the files in his desk drawer, his mind going as it often did to the big bust on the Big Island he and his wife, Lei, had brought down three months ago. Their house had burned down as collateral damage of that case, and Lei had lost their first child four months into the pregnancy.

The new house they were building, a simple three bedroom in concrete block, was almost finished. He couldn't wait to be done with spending every non-working moment laboring on the house. The insurance hadn't paid out enough to rebuild, so they'd had to rely on the help of friends and co-workers, which didn't make for speedy construction.

Stevens felt like he'd been slogging through molasses ever since that Big Island case. Every day seemed to take superhuman effort to get through, and he wondered if he could be suffering some sort of depression or if it was just grief over the fire and losing their baby. It seemed to him that they'd both been operating on autopilot. The only person that really made them smile was his son, Kiet. Kiet, at seven months, was happy and active, always crawling to grab something and put it in his mouth, jade-colored eyes sparkling with curiosity and humor.

Stevens's station closing down hadn't helped his mood. He wasn't looking forward to developing a training program that didn't yet exist, when he wasn't enthusiastic about the changes or sure they would work.

In the past, candidates for detective studied, passed the test, and then worked closely for six months with a "mentor partner" until they were ready to take their own cases. It was a time-tested process.

Now the dictate had come down from central on Oahu that they needed to have procedural standardization to reduce variability in case write-ups and other errors that had plagued departments statewide.

Stevens finished his sorting and looked up as his small team filed into his office.

"Hey guys. I have Omura's new assignments for you." He read off their names and new assignments, allowing the groans and teasing that erupted at some of the assignments. "Just pack your personal stuff. Department furnishings are going into storage."

The group was returning to the main room, grumbling side conversations going on that Stevens pretended not to hear, when Brandon Mahoe, one of his trainees now doing a turn at the watch desk, knocked on the doorjamb.

"Someone here to see you, sir. Says she's your mother."

Download *Rip Tides* and continue reading now!

ACKNOWLEDGMENTS

Aloha dear Readers!

I can't thank you enough for being the encouraging cheer squad you are! Those of you who follow me on Facebook were particularly helpful as I neared the end of this latest roller-coaster ride and felt...well, kind of like how Lei and Stevens must feel—exhausted, flat, worn-out from all the battles.

I know I can't leave Lei and Stevens in that gray zone, or hang out there for long myself, so it's on to the next one. You guys were so great helping me generate new ideas for titles! So next up is _Rip Tides_, Paradise Crime Mystery #9. This will be dealing with a subculture of Hawaii I'm particularly fond of: the surf scene!

I want to thank my awesome expert consultants: Captain David Spicer (Ret), who keeps Lei's police work semi-accurate. Deputy fire chief and fire marshal, San Jose Fire Department (Ret), David Schoonover, was a huge help, sitting me down for a fascinating tutorial on arson investigation and the psychology of arson. He sent tons of articles, too, and read the manuscript for errors! Any flubs that remain are my fault entirely.

I also thank Paul Haake, captain, Fire Prevention Bureau, Department of Fire and Public Safety for Maui County, for promptly and courteously responding to my inquiries about police and arson investigation procedure in Hawaii. Arson and fire science were a completely new area for me, and while I'd been following the arson fires that happen periodically here on Maui and wondering about them, his information about how investigation is done was invaluable.

As always, thanks to my beta readers Bonny Ponting and Noelle Pierce for your discerning eyes and enthusiastic thumbs-up this go-around!

If you liked the story, *please leave a review*. It's the best thanks you can give any author!

Much aloha,

FREE BOOKS

Join my mystery and romance lists and receive free, full-length, award-winning novels *Torch Ginger & Somewhere on St. Thomas.*

tobyneal.net/TNNews

TOBY'S BOOKSHELF

PARADISE CRIME SERIES

Paradise Crime Mysteries
Blood Orchids
Torch Ginger
Black Jasmine
Broken Ferns
Twisted Vine
Shattered Palms
Dark Lava
Fire Beach
Rip Tides
Bone Hook
Red Rain
Bitter Feast

Paradise Crime Mystery
Special Agent Marcella Scott
Stolen in Paradise

Paradies Crime Suspense Mysteries
Unsound

Paradise Crime Thrillers
Wired In
Wired Rogue
Wired Hard
Wired Dark
Wired Dawn
Wired Justice
Wired Secret
Wired Fear
Wired Courage
Wired Truth

ROMANCES

The Somewhere Series
Somewhere on St. Thomas
Somewhere in the City
Somewhere in California

Standalone
Somewhere on Maui

Co-Authored Romance Thrillers
The Scorch Series
Scorch Road
Cinder Road
Smoke Road
Burnt Road
Flame Road
Smolder Road

YOUNG ADULT

Standalone
Island Fire

NONFICTION

Memoir
Freckled

ABOUT THE AUTHOR

Kirkus Reviews calls Neal's writing, *"persistently riveting. Masterly."*

Award-winning, USA Today bestselling social worker turned author Toby Neal grew up on the island of Kaua`i in Hawaii. Neal is a mental health therapist, a career that has informed the depth and complexity of the characters in her stories. Neal's mysteries and thrillers explore the crimes and issues of Hawaii from the bottom of the ocean to the top of volcanoes. Fans call her stories, *"Immersive, addicting, and the next best thing to being there."*

Neal also pens romance, romantic thrillers, and writes memoir/non-fiction under TW Neal.

Visit tobyneal.net for more ways to stay in touch!
or
Join my Facebook readers group, *Friends Who Like Toby Neal Books,* for special giveaways and perks.

Made in the USA
Coppell, TX
28 August 2021

61372401R00142